Cocktails & Laughter

Cocktails & Laughter

THE ALBUMS OF LOELIA LINDSAY
(Loelia, Duchess of Westminster)

Cocktails and Laughter,
But what comes after?
Nobody knows.
Sir Noël Coward, 'Poor Little Rich Girl', from On with the dance

The ancient and now forgotten pastime of high jinks
Sir Walter Scott, 'Guy Mannering

Edited by Hugo Vickers

HAMISH HAMILTON
LONDON

First published in Great Britain 1983
by Hamish Hamilton Ltd
Garden House 57–59 Long Acre London WC2E 9JZ

Introduction copyright © 1983 by Hugo Vickers
Captions to photographs copyright © 1983 by Loelia Lindsay

Book design by David Fordham

British Library Cataloguing in Publication Data

Westminster, Loeila Mary Grosvenor, *Duchess* of
    Cocktails and laughter.
    1. Photography—Portraits
    2. Upper classes—England—Pictorial works
    I. Title   II. Vickers, Hugo
    779′.2′0924   TR681.U/
    ISBN 0–241–11083–1

Filmset by Northumberland Press Ltd, Gateshead
Printed in Great Britain by
Fletcher & Son Ltd, Norwich, Norfolk

CONTENTS

DEDICATION

For Ronnie, Jacynth and Oliver

Loelia's bookplate designed by Rex Whistler.

HUGH RICHARD ARTHUR
DUKE OF WESTMINSTER
1899

Bendor's Book Plate

LOELIA LINDSAY

by

Hugo Vickers

"There was a noisy lunch party at Pam Berry's" recorded Noel Coward in 1957. "Loelia, Annie [Fleming], Virginia Cowles, the ubiquitous Malcolm Muggeridge, whom I can't stand, and Patrick Kinross. It was quite funny and everyone shrieked at once. If the dialogue had been transcribed the critics undoubtedly would have stated confidently that such characters did not exist."

With this in mind and this album in prospect, I decided to tape-record a luncheon at Loelia Lindsay's house. I arrived bearing an enormous machine which I described at the time as "another ear at the table". The guests were Lady Diana Cooper, her grand-daughter, Artemis, and Loelia's niece, Carolyn Ponsonby. While the machine was rather conspicuous and considerably inhibited the three younger members of the party, Diana and Loelia tended to forget its presence.

The conversation began with a discussion concerning the death of an old friend. They had lived too long and seen too many die to face this in other than a matter of fact manner.

> Diana: *Now ... Is it true that —— is dead?*
> Loelia: *Yes, he's dead. I nearly rang you up but I thought why tell you bad news, not that it is all that bad news, let's face it.*
> Diana: *It's jolly good news.*
> Loelia: *Well, she doesn't take quite that line.*
> Diana: *Well, I take that line.*

> Loelia: *I take that line too. But I don't think it's the right thing to say. You say: "I do understand you are feeling rather sad." That is the line.*
> Diana: *How did he die?*
> Loelia: *He died in really rather a strange way ....*

The manner of his departing was then described in considerable detail, the death itself registering on tape as a click of the fingers, followed by silence.

> Diana: *Well, this morning the news was broken to me as "not to be relied upon".*
> Loelia: *What? That he's dead? You can rely on me, I promise. Ab-so-lutely!*
> Diana: *I'm afraid I said, "How wonderful!"*

During the lunch itself, the "extra ear" coped admirably with the slower conversation, punctuated with the sound of knives and forks on plates. What was especially fascinating was that the machine caught nuances which escaped me at the time. Listening to it alone later, I realised how skilfully Loelia brought us all into the conversation in turn, and how, once we were drawn in, we then stayed in, and general conversation was established. I learned for the first time that there is an art in entertaining beyond good food and carefully chosen guests. Diana had been talking of her wartime visit to Shwe Dagôn in Rangoon, and saying with pride that she had had to remove not only her shoes but also her stockings. Conscious of the wish to give the tape every chance, Artemis had been silent. Loelia drew her firmly in with the line: "Artemis, have you ever been asked to peel off your tights to go into some sacrosanct spot?"

After lunch there came a discussion about the Windsors, who though contemporaries of Diana's, have already faded into the pages of history.

Loelia: *Now I tell you what I wanted to ask you, Diana. What about the Windsors? Because you're so into the Windsors, aren't you?*

Diana: *Yes.*

Loelia: *I always remember a great schism as to whether people should curtsey to the Duchess or not. You were one of the ones who sank to the ground.*

Diana: *Yes. Well, I only went to the ground to please him.*

Loelia: *Well, of course. You were perfectly right. I remember when they were at Sunningdale when all her jewellery was removed from her, poor Duchess, I had them over for cocktails at the end of the war. I had a few people staying and I drilled them beforehand and said: "Remember now, you've all got to curtsey to him but not to her." I'm frightfully flustered introducing people, that kind of thing. I shake hands warmly with him and sink to the floor with her. The other guests all glare at me. Did you like her?*

Diana: *I was never what's called intimate.*

Loelia: *No, one couldn't have been. I don't think it was on.*

Diana: *And people think I was. But I was never a bit intimate.*

Loelia: *Were you intimate with him?*

Diana: *No. Neither. No question of intimacy ever. On the other hand she was great fun. But hard as nails, really hard as nails.*

Loelia: *I thought she was too animated. She was more than lively. Everything worked and twitched all over her face. Every muscle, every eyelash and she put her face rather near to one.*

Diana: *And wisecracks.*

Loelia: *Yes, wisecracks. Very American, of course.*

Diana: *Very.*

Loelia: *No, I don't know whether I liked her or not. I didn't like him much either.*

Diana: *I never was fond of her. I don't know anyone who was. Perhaps the aunt, Aunt Bessie?*

Loelia: *The aunt! I went to the house in Baltimore and I paid my dollar. I was going from New York to Washington when I saw the train stopped at Baltimore. So, with this friend of mine who was a sporting character too, I said: "Come on, let's hurl ourselves into a taxi and see where Wallis comes from!" So we were just able to do it in time. We went off to this appalling little house in a very minor street, it might have been in a seaside town, a row of ghastly little houses and there it was. You paid a dollar to go in and you could be photographed in the bath-tub for another dollar.*

Diana: *In the bath-tub?*

Loelia: *Yes, it cost you another dollar.*

Diana: *To strip?*

Loelia: *I don't know. I didn't pay. The only thing I do remember is that this ghastly little house had what they call a well, which means that there's a room in front on the first floor and then a passage and a room at the back. The middle bit is called a well. And you peer over the bannisters and see what's going on in the hall. On the bannister was a plaque on which was written "This is where Aunt Bessie kept an eye on Wallis and her beaux". Can you beat it? Well worth a dollar.*

While the Windsors have faded away, one by death and the other by a decade of illness, both Diana and Loelia have survived to take an active part in the 1980s, have had to learn to cope with answering machines and other gadgets that are a part of modern life. Born in the age of elaborate hats, parasols and horse-drawn carriages, they have lived long enough to welcome take away foods and driving themselves about in their own little cars. Loelia is now grateful for one live-in couple, who between them fulfil the roles of cook and maid, butler, chauffeur and gardener. Loelia's life is a twentieth-century life, and she has spent most of its decades right in the centre of the stage.

Loelia was born in 1902, the only daughter of Sir Frederick Ponsonby, later Lord Sysonby. Sir Frederick's father, General Sir Henry Ponsonby, took part in the Crimean War and was for twenty-five years Private Secretary to Queen Victoria. He and his wife, Mary Bulteel, formerly a Maid of Honour to the Queen, resided in Windsor Castle for thirty-four years. Every Sunday as the Military Knights of Windsor march out of St. George's Chapel, they face the memorial tablet placed in the Chapel by Sir Frederick and his brothers. Of Sir Henry, Elizabeth Longford, Queen Victoria's biographer, wrote: 'For thirty years he was to pepper Queen Victoria with liberal ideas and spice her court with humour. What the *Greville Memoirs* do for the first half of Queen Victoria's reign the Ponsonby Letters do for the second."[1]

Sir Frederick followed his father into royal service, beginning as Equerry and Assistant Private Secretary to Queen Victoria in 1895. Likewise he served Edward VII and George V, who appointed him Keeper of the Privy Purse in 1914 and Treasurer in 1920. He has been described as "a courtier to his fingertips" whose "devotion to the Royal Family was absolutely genuine".[2] He saw one of his most important roles as to keep the Sovereign in touch with public opinion. He was polite, inscrutable and an excellent linguist and he relished all matters of etiquette and ceremonial. Like all the Royal Family, he could detect any error of uniform or medal. King George V relied on him greatly and was profoundly shocked by his sudden death in Silver Jubilee Year. Sir Frederick's book, *Recollections of Three Reigns*, was published in 1951 and is full of fascinating anecdotes about life in royal service, considerably more interesting than the trivia produced by today's royal biographers.

Though Sir Frederick was loved and respected by most members of the Royal Family, the Kaiser was not amongst them. He never forgave Sir Frederick for publishing his mother's letters in 1928. And his daughter, Princess Victoria, Duchess of Brunswick, devoted six pages of her memoirs to an attempt to blacken Sir Frederick's name.

Loelia lived at St. James's Palace and, though it is wrong to suggest that she was brought up with the royal children, she was certainly aware of them from an early age. She once sat on Edward VII's lap and made him laugh by seizing his beard and asking him: "But King, where's your crown?" She spent a summer at Park House, Sandringham (now famous as the birthplace of Lady Diana Spencer), and several summers at Birkhall, previously occupied by Queen Alexandra's redoubtable old Comptroller, Sir Dighton Probyn, V.C. Sir Dighton had a long white beard and his chin nested on his breast. In uniform he was a magnificent figure, the thickness of his splendid beard hiding most of his decorations, including his Victoria Cross. Loelia has a wonderful story of Queen Alexandra wishing to give her old friend an eightieth birthday treat. The Queen took him to the Croydon Air Show to see the display. Alas, Sir Dighton was unable to look up and had to be laid on his back to enjoy the fun.

Loelia's childhood had all the possibilities of being idyllic but it was far from that. She suffered a string of dreadful foreign governesses, the worst of whom used to drag a comb through her hair to cause pain, hold her head under water in a basin, and, on discovering that she was afraid of the dark, oblige her to go through empty rooms in her old Tudor home, full of dust-sheet covered furniture, which soon magnified into ghostly shapes in her imagination.

Unfortunate scrapes with royalty can have done little to give her confidence. One year at the Ghillies' Ball at Balmoral, the Ladies of the Household decided to kiss Queen Mary's hand as they curtsied to her. They explained to Loelia the correct etiquette for this manoeuvre. She told the story in her memoirs:

When my turn came I seized Queen Mary's hand and pressed it ardently to my lips — to perceive immediately that I had left a perfect print of a scarlet mouth on the back of her white kid glove. She gave me a withering look that said all and I slunk away in disgrace, praying that my family had not noticed my faux pas.[3]

1. *Victoria R. I.* by Elizabeth Longford (Weidenfeld & Nicolson 1964) p. 324.
2. *Recollections of Three Reigns* by Sir Frederick Ponsonby (Eyre & Spottiswoode 1957) Introduction p. x.
3. *Grace and Favour* by Loelia, Duchess of Westminster (Weidenfeld & Nicolson 1961) p. 104.

In those days girls suddenly left their childhood and adolescence by "coming out". They were meant to emerge overnight from a chrysalis, a gorgeous butterfly, equipped with every social grace, to be thrown into the grown-up world of dinner-parties and balls. The kind of men encountered at such dinners were hardly of the type to inspire confidence. Caught between two young bloods, deeply preoccupied with conversation about racing and gambling, the last vestige of Loelia's confidence vanished when she observed her mother mouthing the words "talk, talk" across the table.

Clearly the subject of shyness was to preoccupy Loelia, because during our collaboration I found some notes she had written later in life, entitled "Hints for the Shy". Even years later she was writing: "Edwardian children were brought up in such an atmosphere of suppression that every iota of self-confidence was squashed out of them. Then at the age of eighteen, these pathetic debutantes were supposed to dazzle all and sundry". Loelia learned to cope with this agonizing situation by painful experience. Here is her advice:

1) If you have to enter a room full of terrifying elders and you are quaking at the knees, walk slowly. It is fatal to bustle in. You only look foolish and ungainly and probably you will knock something over, thus drawing more attention to yourself. A slow and stately walk belies your nervous state.

2) However much uphill work is involved and however boring and uninspiring your conversation with your neighbour at dinner may be, always look him straight in the eye. He will easily be mugged into believing he is fascinating you. This is also quite a good wheeze when you want to listen in to a fascinating conversation at the other end of the table. Your dinner partner can be fooled into believing you are enthralled by his tedious talk if you only avert your mind and not your gaze. Two good topics when you are really stuck are ghosts and the Royal Family.

3) If you are surrounded by a lot of glamorous girls of your own age but feel you cannot compete with them (and the numbers are even) remember when your hostess announces "All
sit wherever you please", choose the most glamorous girl and quickly sit one seat away from her. In that way you will have one side covered. There is nothing more humiliating than to wait until every seat is occupied except the two on either side of you. I know!

Finally, Loelia adds a warning:

When you have conquered your shyness (which you will), guard against becoming too shrill and assertive. It can happen.

Loelia was fortunate enough to move away from her parents somewhat narrow set into a much livelier group, now remembered as "The Bright Young People". Lady Eleanor Smith and the Jungman sisters, Zita and Teresa (then always known as Baby), were the ringleaders, assisted by another friend, Enid Raphael. The pranks they got up to are harmless enough in retrospect, but shocked the grown-ups at the time. Years later Zita wrote to Loelia: "The terrible things we did are boomeranging on us now. I can't help feeling that your mother must have regretted the circumstances that brought us together, she must have thought us horrid, and our goings on intensely vulgar. *We* enjoyed it, of course."

These four girls invented the treasure hunts (which Loelia describes later) and they used to dress sixteen-year-old Teresa as a Russian spy, named Anna Worolski, and set her loose on unsuspecting young men with a mysterious story of hidden Russian jewels. Sometimes they pretended to be reporters from non-existent newspapers and called on film-stars to interview them. Teresa once interviewed Beverley Nichols at Claridge's, while Zita and Eleanor hid under the table. Today Zita says the diaries she kept in those days are filled with references to everyone "screaming" with joy: "We were all so over-excited. We were all talking about ourselves always." Loelia's special contribution was to invent the bottle-party in 1926, an innocent and sensible enough arrangement to give a party on the cheap, which, as she says, became improbably "the ancestor of many a squalid, law-evading, orgy".

The Twenties are also remembered as the Night-Club age. "Of course I went to the Embassy whenever I got the chance . . . it was like going to a lovely party where one knew everyone."

At other times the young of the day amused themselves with pencil and paper games and Consequences. The success of these depended on the company.

Charades were also popular at practically every house-party. The guests threw themselves into it heart and soul. The real professionals had words of two syllables sustained over three acts. And dressing-up of course was the great delight. Cecil Beaton and Oliver Messel staged elaborate fancy-dress pageants, while at weekends nobody's wardrobe was safe. Dowagers would have been considered very unsporting if they had objected to finding their feather boas draped round Oliver Messel's neck.

A chance meeting was to change all this. A dull evening ended unexpectedly in a wildly successful party at the Duke of Westminster's London home, Bourdon House, with Hutch singing and a lavish supper laid out in the dining room, all at a moment's notice. The Duke, a dashing, legendary figure, was as struck with Loelia as she was with him and she was soon being courted in the most romantic way. Exotic flowers would arrive daily. The Duke proved an ingenious present-giver. On the way to Venice, they stopped off in Paris and Loelia left a felt hat in a bedroom. Collecting it later, she found a large diamond clip pinned to it. Later again, on opening her suitcase, a platinum powder box with ribbons of sapphires and diamonds met her eye. She went to sleep in her sleeper and awoke with a hard lump digging into her. It was a diamond and emerald brooch. Next day, searching in her handbag for her passport, a diamond and ruby bracelet emerged. They married in 1930 in a blaze of publicity with Winston Churchill as Best Man.

The Duke (who was born in 1879) was known as Bendor, because his grandfather had won the Derby with a famous horse called *Bend Or*. As a young officer in the Royal Horse Guards he was ADC to Lord Milner and to Field Marshal Lord Roberts. He served in the South African War and in World War I. He had already been married twice, first to "Sheelagh" Cornwallis-West. He was divorced by Sheelagh in 1919 and married

Violet Rowley (now Mrs Violet Cripps). This marriage also ended in divorce, in 1926.

A number of people have described him. Anita Leslie saw him when she was young:

.... Bendor showed himself good-natured and petulant by turn. I liked him, but he obviously did not know where to turn next for diversion. He needed to work in some leper colony to get his priorities right and discover himself. As it was, he fretted amidst toadies who were ready to dash off to Norway with him for the fishing, or to the South of France for the sun, but within hours he would change his mind and then appear cross with himself and everyone else. Yet how could this man have struggled out of the net he was born into? My father was fond of him. Bendor took him off for long confidences to complain of the lack of true romance, saying he was "tired of handing out pearl necklaces".[4]

And Chips Channon wrote at the time of his death in 1953:

So Bend Or the great Duke of Westminster is dead at last; magnificent, courteous, a mixture of Henry VIII and Lorenzo Il Magnifico, he lived for pleasure – and women – for 74 years. His wealth was incalculable; his charm overwhelming; but he was restless, spoilt, irritable, and rather splendid in a very English way. He was fair, handsome, lavish; yet his life was an empty failure; he did few kindnesses, leaves no monument.[5]

Loelia herself has left a very fair portrait of him in her memoirs. She told me that, when he travelled, "the Emperor of Russia couldn't have had more luxury". There was an occasion at the Hotel Lotti in Paris when the Duke wanted a peach at two in the morning. It was so late that the young waiter sent out to find one encountered great difficulties. There was no question of his returning empty-handed for he knew he would lose his job. Finally he broke a shop window and stole one. The young waiter became famous in later life as George Orwell, author of *1984*. Accustomed to such treatment it is not surprising that

4. *The Gilt and The Gingerbread* by Anita Leslie (Hutchinson 1981) p. 133.
5. *Chips. The Diaries of Sir Henry Channon* (Weidenfeld & Nicolson 1967) p. 477.

Bendor was spoilt. Sadly, he also displayed a cruelly jealous streak. His wife was scared of him and could make no plans of her own however small. The Duke's "every passing whim" had to be obeyed. He told her he preferred the company of what he called "Real People", by which he meant obscure people. He veered from being wholly charming at one moment and a man of rage the next. After nearly five years they parted. In 1947 they were divorced. The jewels were sold.

Many of the photographs in this album cover the period in which Loelia recreated a life for herself, first in rented houses and then in 1940 at Send Grove in Surrey. Here she entertained a great deal. James Lees-Milne has described the house and its atmosphere:

Send is an enchanting small Jane Austen house, symmetrical, stuccoed and washed pink. The front is covered by an enormous wisteria. It dates from the end of the eighteenth century. The prospect from the house covers a long expanse of grass, with curving boundary to the left, and to the right open views across a river bordered with pollarded willows in the direction of Clandon. . . . My hostess has impeccable taste. She bought this house a year after the war when it was not too late to buy French wall papers. As you enter there is a charming little stairwell with a ballustered staircase cork-screwing steeply upwards towards a domed ceiling. To the right and left are projecting bays forming a small dining-room and boudoir. Beyond the boudoir is a library with coffered ceiling. The bookcases in this room appear to be late eighteenth century. I arrived late and rather flummoxed. The duchess greeted me at the dining-room door, napkin in hand. I washed and joined the party straight away. A delicious dinner at a small round table. After dinner we talked in the library about Keats and Shelley. . . .[6]

Loelia travelled whenever the opportunity arose, and this album includes some pictures of Ian Fleming and life at Goldeneye. It may not be well known that one of Ian Fleming's semi-private jokes was to name characters in James Bond books after his friends. Thus "Shady"

Tree was called after Michael Tree, Ronald Tree's son, "Tiffany" Case after Margaret Case of *Vogue*. An American businessman in the book is recognised by the name on his brief-case: B Kitteridge, in real life the late Oxford loving millionaire, Ben Kitteridge, and so on. In early editions of *Diamonds are Forever*, Bond's secretary was called Loelia Ponsonby and even after Ian Fleming changed the name to Miss Moneypenny, Bond addressed her as "Lil" and not "Moneypenny" as in the film. "Lil" was the name by which Ian Fleming always addressed Loelia.

Needlework became an absorbing passion. Loelia had always enjoyed sewing and one day at Eaton was stitching away in the drawing-room. Her father said "What are you making? A pair of knickers, I suppose." This proved correct. "Why don't you make something worthwhile like an altar-cloth?" he suggested. (Many years later she did.) After turning to more imaginative needlework, she found that her particular speciality was what she calls "Painting in beads". She began by planting the occasional bead in a flower or a leaf, but eventually the beads took over. Canvas was replaced by satin and she created flower-pictures made of beads. As her work became known, the Royal School of Needlework invited her to co-judge a competition. Ernest Thesiger, the well-known actor, was the other judge. They disagreed on almost every point but, at tea later, he asked her in a somewhat patronising tone what she was working on. It transpired that he had been given a large box of beads, but had never known what to do with them. He offered to send them. When eventually they arrived, they turned out to be an extraordinary treasure-trove: pill boxes, test tubes with cork stoppers, and old cough drop tins revealed a collection of beads about a hundred years old with every grade of colour. Thus if Loelia started to work on a dusky mauve rose she had perhaps twenty shades to choose from. Some of the beads were too small and delicate even for her expert hands, and most of them are unobtainable today.

One picture in her drawing-room today is often taken for a pen and ink sketch of Send Grove, but in fact contains not one drawn line. It is worked in three silks, black, dark grey and pale grey. In order to make the

---

6. *Ancestral Voices* by James Lees-Milne (Chatto & Windus 1975) pp. 229–30.

sky look lighter, the cloud outlines are worked in hairs from her own head. Unlike eighteenth-century ladies who had very long hair, Loelia was only able to obtain five or six stitches per hair, which proves that one of the golden rules of needlework is patience. The other is that at all times the highest possible standards must be maintained. Unsatisfactory results must be un-picked. Loelia's needlework has been exhibited on many occasions. Eventually her collection will be put on permanent display at one of the National Trust's smaller country houses. Of this she is justifiably proud.

In 1961 Loelia published her memoirs, *Grace and Favour*. At that time she had a flat in Grosvenor Square and presently she received a letter from an admiring reader who lived op-posite. This was Sir Martin Lindsay of Dowhill, well known as an explorer in the Arctic and a former Conservative M.P. For a month she left the letter unanswered, wondering if she wanted to meet the unknown admirer. Eventually they did meet and in 1969 they married, an unexpected and happy marriage which lasted until Sir Martin's death in 1981.

Today Loelia lives in a small cottage on the Send estate, previously the home of the gardener. The house was converted to imagina-tive designs by Loelia herself. Flowered wall-papers were specially painted for the rooms, and the spiral stairs that led to the first floor are particularly ingenious. The carpet is done in needlework, step by step, so that worn patches can easily be reworked. The design shows the sea tumbling down, bringing in its wake coral and pearls and shells. The bottom step has a bottle bobbing in the waves with Loelia's signa-ture inside it. The walls have shells on them and in the hall is a mirror she made herself with a sea-blue frame and any number of beautiful shells brought back from her Australian trip. The idea of the sea is even extended to the special flooring in the hall. The blocks of the floor give the impression of shingle.

The garden outside was a rubbish-heap when Loelia arrived and the first thing to be done was to bring in a bulldozer and clear it. In the bad winter of 1963 Loelia surveyed the scene and so messy was it that the mud oozed over the top of her Wellington boots. Now the garden gives Loelia perhaps her greatest satisfaction. Her daily routine involves several hours of work in it, and in the summer she sometimes allows herself the pleasure of sitting in it observing the flowers around her. A favourite idea is to have roses climbing as high as possible up trees. Thus, in season, white roses tumble over the green trees in waterfalls. Flowers also abound in the house, cymbidiums and lilies being particular favourites. By careful planning in the small greenhouse Loelia never has to resort to buying flowers for the house at any time in the year.

Though once married to London's richest landlord, she owns no property in the capital and only goes there occasionally to see friends or attend the opera. From time to time she has broadcast or appeared on television and in 1982 she suddenly found herself portrayed on stage by Lucy Fleming in a play called *A Private Affair*. A few years ago she produced a privately-printed anthology of favourite poems and epigrams. Most often quoted today is her alarming adage: "Anybody seen in a bus over the age of thirty has been a failure in life." Having acquired something of a follow-ing after the publication of her memoirs, a BBC talk entitled "I Remember" brought in a further flood of letters. Loelia had spoken of governesses and for one reader this struck a painful note:

> *It brought back to me so vividly many memories of my own young days, as we also had a shocking German governess, so unkind that a meeting was held in the nursery to offer prayers that she might be removed, one brother having said that he did not wish to go to Heaven if she was likely to be there too.*

It is in the hope that happier memories will be evoked that Loelia turned recently to her albums to select the photographs that follow. For this reason one or two of the albums' inmates had to be rejected: "I won't have him. He's a dreadful bore. Put him in the Bores' Derby and he'd win by ten lengths", or, "Not her. She's a Horror from Horrorville". In presenting these pictures she seeks only to illustrate how things were from the point of view of one who lived through those times and was lucky enough to know a wide variety of talented, glamorous and sometimes eccentric characters.

THE PONSONBYS

PRO·REGE·LEGE·GREGE

The Ponsonby origins are somewhat vague but it is known that they came from Picardy and arrived in England with the Plantagenets. It is possible that one of them held the office of Hereditary Barber and Surgeon to Henry II, a theory made more believable because the Ponsonbys have three combs emblazoned on their shield. In which case it is nice to think he might have run into the "Grand Master of the King's Hounds" or *Gros Veneur*, from whom it is suggested the Grosvenors descend, but this may well be stretching a number of myths too far. The first well documented Ponsonby was Sir John, a Roundhead who raised a regiment of Horse for Oliver Cromwell. He accompanied Cromwell to Ireland and established a new family there, confiscating land at will and calling it Bessborough. The 3rd Earl of Bessborough descends directly from him. He married Lady Henrietta Spencer, daughter of the 1st Earl Spencer, so Loelia is thus a fourth cousin once removed of the Princess of Wales. Major-General the Hon. Sir Frederick Ponsonby, her great-grandfather, fought at Waterloo. His son, Sir Henry, served in the Crimea and Canada and for the last twenty-five years of his life was the devoted Private Secretary to Queen Victoria. Sir Henry married one of the Queen's maids of honour, Mary Bulteel, a grand-daughter of Lady Grey. Besides two daughters, Albertha and Magdalen, the marriage produced three sons, Major-General Sir John, Sir Frederick (later Lord Sysonby, and Loelia's father), and Arthur, an M.P. who was created Lord Ponsonby of Shullbrede. Arthur wrote various books including a book about his father, *Henry Ponsonby: His Life from his Letters*, published by Macmillan in 1942.

Another interesting Ponsonby was Loelia's ancestral aunt, better known as Lady Caroline Lamb, who became infatuated with Byron and after he grew tired of her fell victim to fits of deep melancholy and violent temper. She also wrote several novels. One of these, *Glenarvon*, published anonymously in 1816, contains a bitter pen-portrait of Byron.

SIR JOHN
PONSONBY = Mary Robley
(*1866–1952*)

MAGDALEN
(*1864–1934*)

VICTOR
(*b & d 1900*)

SELECT PONSONBY TREE

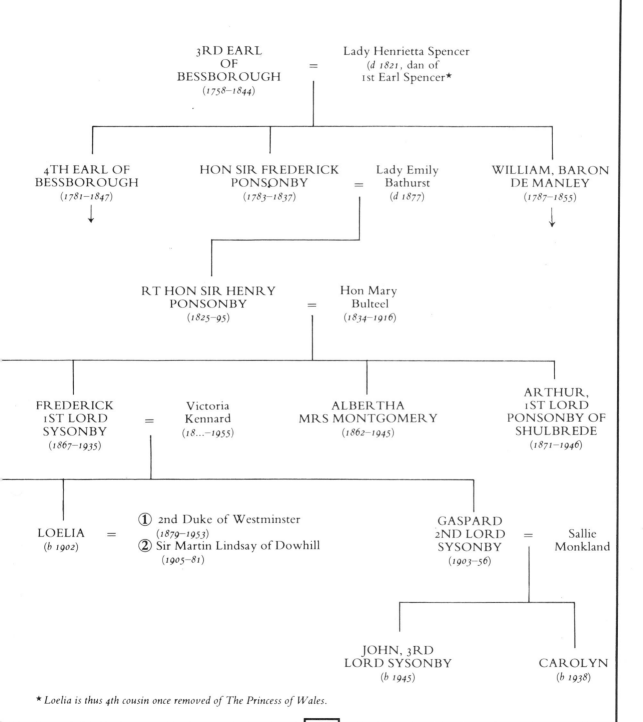

3RD EARL OF BESSBOROUGH (1758–1844) = Lady Henrietta Spencer (d 1821, dan of 1st Earl Spencer★)

4TH EARL OF BESSBOROUGH (1781–1847)

HON SIR FREDERICK PONSONBY (1783–1837) = Lady Emily Bathurst (d 1877)

WILLIAM, BARON DE MANLEY (1787–1855)

RT HON SIR HENRY PONSONBY (1825–95) = Hon Mary Bulteel (1834–1916)

FREDERICK 1ST LORD SYSONBY (1867–1935) = Victoria Kennard (18...–1955)

ALBERTHA MRS MONTGOMERY (1862–1945)

ARTHUR, 1ST LORD PONSONBY OF SHULBREDE (1871–1946)

LOELIA (b 1902) = ① 2nd Duke of Westminster (1879–1953) ② Sir Martin Lindsay of Dowhill (1905–81)

GASPARD 2ND LORD SYSONBY (1903–56) = Sallie Monkland

JOHN, 3RD LORD SYSONBY (b 1945)

CAROLYN (b 1938)

★ *Loelia is thus 4th cousin once removed of The Princess of Wales.*

THE DUKES OF WESTMINSTER

VIRTUS · NON · STEMMA

There can be no more curious succession than that of the Westminster Dukedom. The first Duke's heir died in his lifetime so he was succeeded by his grandson, Bendor. Bendor's only son died aged four. Bendor's heir after that was his uncle, Arthur, who died in 1929, and then Arthur's son, Robert, who pre-deceased his cousin by a mere five weeks. Robert's son, Hugh, had been accidentally killed in 1947, so, on Bendor's death, the title passed to William, the unmarried son of his other uncle Henry. William, the 3rd Duke, died in 1963 and the title passed to the descendants of the 1st Duke by his second wife, Katherine. Lord Hugh Grosvenor had been killed in the First World War, but his son, Gerald, succeeded as 4th Duke. He had no children so, on his death, his brother Robert became the 5th Duke. Robert died in 1979, and his son, Gerald, is the present Duke. At the time of writing, he only has daughters and there is therefore no heir to the Dukedom at the moment. In the event of the present Duke's death, the Marquessate of Westminster and other lesser titles pass to the Earl of Wilton, whose heir is yet another cousin, Lord Ebury, who resides in Melbourne, Australia.

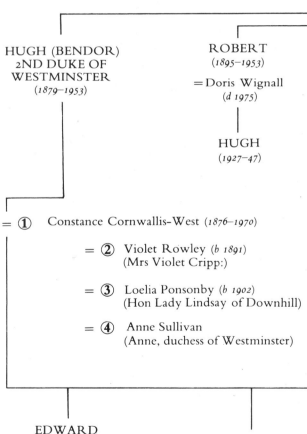

HUGH (BENDOR) 2ND DUKE OF WESTMINSTER (1879–1953)

ROBERT (1895–1953)
= Doris Wignall (d 1975)
HUGH (1927–47)

= ① Constance Cornwallis-West (1876–1970)
= ② Violet Rowley (b 1891) (Mrs Violet Cripp:)
= ③ Loelia Ponsonby (b 1902) (Hon Lady Lindsay of Downhill)
= ④ Anne Sullivan (Anne, duchess of Westminster)

EDWARD EARL GROSVENOR (1904–9)

LADY MARY (b 1910)

SELECT WESTMINSTER TREE

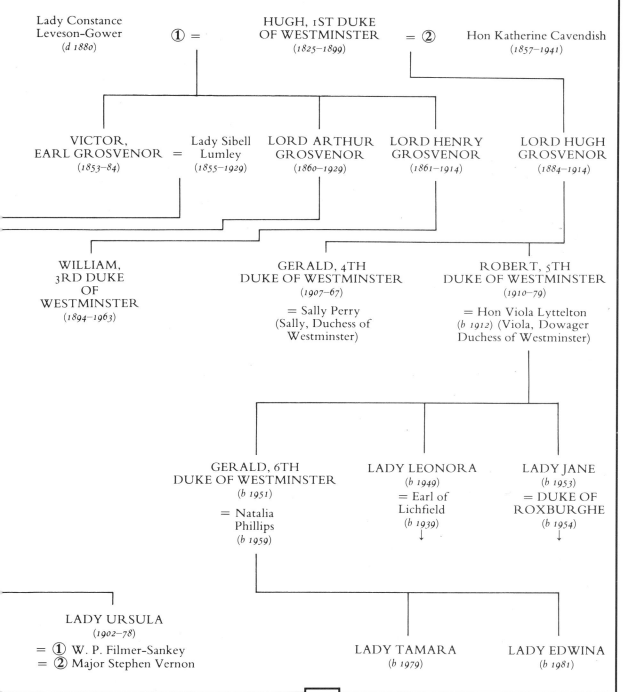

Lady Constance
Leveson-Gower
(d 1880)

① =

HUGH, 1ST DUKE
OF WESTMINSTER
(1825–1899)

= ②

Hon Katherine Cavendish
(1857–1941)

VICTOR,
EARL GROSVENOR
(1853–84)

=

Lady Sibell
Lumley
(1855–1929)

LORD ARTHUR
GROSVENOR
(1860–1929)

LORD HENRY
GROSVENOR
(1861–1914)

LORD HUGH
GROSVENOR
(1884–1914)

WILLIAM,
3RD DUKE
OF
WESTMINSTER
(1894–1963)

GERALD, 4TH
DUKE OF WESTMINSTER
(1907–67)

= Sally Perry
(Sally, Duchess of
Westminster)

ROBERT, 5TH
DUKE OF WESTMINSTER
(1910–79)

= Hon Viola Lyttelton
(b 1912) (Viola, Dowager
Duchess of Westminster)

GERALD, 6TH
DUKE OF WESTMINSTER
(b 1951)

= Natalia
Phillips
(b 1959)

LADY LEONORA
(b 1949)
= Earl of
Lichfield
(b 1939)
↓

LADY JANE
(b 1953)
= DUKE OF
ROXBURGHE
(b 1954)
↓

LADY URSULA
(1902–78)
= ① W. P. Filmer-Sankey
= ② Major Stephen Vernon

LADY TAMARA
(b 1979)

LADY EDWINA
(b 1981)

My grandmother, Mary Bulteel, one of Queen Victoria's Maids of Honour until she married Sir Henry Ponsonby. She can never have been a beauty as she had a long upper lip which she bequeathed to her children, but she had a clever face and was very charming. Besides being a good wife and mother, she followed artistic, literary and musical pursuits. She was interested in social problems and active in liberal causes. She was a life-long friend of the Empress Frederick and Queen Victoria also liked her, though she suspected her of being not only clever but in league with the Radicals and thus a sinister influence on her husband.

*M*y mother was a great beauty and was expected by her parents, who were rich and I suspect rather bourgeois, to make a brilliant match and carry off the Duke of Seven Dials of the day. Instead she got engaged to the penniless second son of Queen Victoria's famous secretary, Sir Henry Ponsonby. Both families were in an uproar and decided to oppose the match at all costs. A powerful adversary joined their embattled ranks in the form of Queen Victoria, who sternly disapproved of any of her courtiers getting married, especially an equerry, which my father was at the time. The lovers were parted for two years, but love triumphed and at the end of the nineteenth century they were betrothed. Queen Victoria, presumably resigned to the match, gave the young couple a silver tea set as a wedding present. Her dresser, while packing this, asked rather bravely, "Don't you think you should add a coffee pot as well?" To which the Queen replied, "Are you giving this present or am I?"

*M*y father was in royal service for over forty years and treasurer to the King for fifteen. He wrote a book about court life called RECOLLECTIONS OF THREE REIGNS which was published after his death in October 1935, shortly before that of King George V.

*G*reat Tangley Manor, near Guildford, was a house
we shared with my Kennard grandfather. Part of it was
very early and reputed to have been King John's
hunting box. A small bit of the wall was said to be
Saxon, very rare as part of the structure of the house. It
was moated and one could still see part of where the
drawbridge had been. When we lived there, it was a
muddle of black and white half-timbering, gables, low
beams, diamond-paned windows and panelling. The
garden had a very old yew hedge and masses of
herbaceous flowers and azaleas which reflected
themselves all around the lake.

The Treasurer to the King
Taken from Life

*T*his is a caricature of my father dressed in the
Windsor uniform and wearing the riband of the Royal
Victorian Order. It was executed by George Belcher,
who was famous for his caricatures of charwomen in
PUNCH.

This photograph of me was taken when I was eleven months old. I seem to be in a Rolls Royce of a pram.

"*A playmate of the Royal Children. The daughter of Captain F. Ponsonby, one of the King's equerries-in-waiting, and the grand daughter of the late Sir Henry Ponsonby, who served Prince Edward's great-grandmother so faithfully for forty years. The child's name is Loelia Mary and she is two years and six months old.*"

Queen Victoria made it as difficult as possible for my parents to have a life together. The equerry on duty was forbidden to leave the grounds of Windsor Castle except on Sundays. My parents therefore bought a farm house a few miles from the Castle gates, and the moment my father was free, he would bicycle off to spend his twenty hours' leave with his beloved. There was very little "va et viens" with the Royal Family. Thus my parents were horrified when this picture of me aged 2½ appeared in the WINDSOR GAZETTE. They feared that the Royal Family would suspect them of having a hand in the dastardly deed of pushing their small daughter into the limelight and pretend she was basking in royal favour. I had of course never met a royal personage in my short life and did not do so for some years to come. What had actually happened was that the "odd man" had found his way into the conservatory with his Brownie camera, and found me rocking away happily. He hit on the idea of taking my picture and selling it to the local paper. I imagine he was sacked with ignomy, while Papa did his best to quell King Edward's wrath.

The Master of the Household
has received Their Majesties' commands
to invite Captain and Mrs T Ponsonby
& their daughter
to a Children's Party at Buckingham Palace on
Thursday the 23rd June 4 to 6.30 o'clock.

Children between 2 and 15 years of age.

Morning Dress.

It is unthinkable today that an invitation to a
Children's Party would bear the instructions "Morning
Dress" but that was how it was in 1904 when this
party took place. I started my first love affair aged two
in the gardens of the Palace. Having become totally
enamoured of a sentry, I spent the entire afternoon
gazing at him with adoring eyes. Several times my
parents retrieved me, but I was back in a flash to swoon
at my beloved.

I was invited to this party in 1908 without my parents.
I was then six years old and I still remember clambering
up the enormous red-carpeted stairs, on my short stout
legs. We played musical chairs and I won by pushing
the future King George VI (then aged twelve), off the
chair with a sharp thrust of my little bottom.

BUCKINGHAM PALACE

PRINCESS MARY hopes that

Miss Loelia Ponsonby.

will come to her small birthday party

at Buckingham Palace from 4 to 7 p.m.

on Saturday, 25th April next.

The reply should be addressed to
The Master of the Household,
Buckingham Palace.

My first genuine encounter with Royalty happened about ten years later in the middle of World War One. For reasons that I cannot imagine, my mother went to the Vosges to run a canteen for the French Army. My father, to his fury, was recalled from France by King George V to run his Household. Perhaps as a recompense for this, he was lent a Grace and Favour house at Sandringham, Park House (now famous as the childhood home of the Princess of Wales). In this particularly hideous house my brother and I were marooned with a skeleton staff for those days of cook, parlour maid and one other. Queen Alexandra lived at Sandringham and she took pity on us "orphaned" children. Several times she took us to her beach chalet at the sea. My brother and I, clad in navy blue costumes trimmed with white (DE RIGUEUR in those days), dashed into the icy grey waves and of course stayed in far too long for our own good. Poor Queen Alexandra called us

frantically from the shore but we odious little brats paid no attention. When we finally emerged, the Queen enveloped us in huge bath towels and dried us down.

My brother paid dearly for this. Shortly afterwards he was struck down by polio. My mother was unreachable, and my father had to leave his dying mother and train up to Wolverhampton, then a private royal station. There I met him in a brougham with two spanking horses.

My brother remained desperately ill for some time and I was often alone. Queen Alexandra, such a tiny elegant little figure, used to come over often to see me. We had difficulty in communicating as she was stone deaf and I was too shy to speak, but I remember the characteristic gestures she made with her hand.

The four smaller figures seen rather unceremoniously with their backs to the camera are (from left to right) Prince Henry (later Duke of Gloucester), Prince George (later Duke of Kent), my brother Gaspard and myself. The picture was taken in 1916. Trout netting on the shores of Lock Muick, near Balmoral, was a yearly treat. The younger members of the party always dashed into the water to help haul in the nets. A French chef, dressed in white cap, would then cook the newly caught fish over a wood fire. King George V and Queen Mary sat on chairs while the rest of us sprawled on the heather and the fish fry was served by royal footmen.

Sometimes we went for walks and picnics with poor little Prince John, Queen Mary's youngest and forgotten child. He was suffering from epilepsy, but children being as they are, we just thought him rather a cissie as, when we climbed Lochnagar, he was attached to his nanny by a long rope. He must have been reasonably tough though as we nearly reached the top of this crag, which has since been made famous by Prince Charles in the fairy story he wrote for his brothers, The Old Man of Lochnagar. Prince John died in 1919. He was only thirteen years old.

My first grown-up get up when I was fifteen. It was brown velvet and my mother bought it in a sale.

The Prince of Wales (later Duke of Windsor) came to Balmoral on leave in 1916. There were more grouse that year than had ever been known before or, I believe, since. And there were not enough guns or beaters to drive them. The Prince of Wales is on the left. Beside him are Prince Henry and Prince George, Sir Godfrey Thomas (the Prince of Wales's Private Secretary) and Mr Henry Hansell, the royal tutor. My brother and I are in the front, behind my father.

Every summer the King loaned Birkhall to my father. Birkhall stands on a mound which sweeps down to the river Dee at the foot of a most delectable garden. I remember a glorious riot of flowers and also what appealed to my brother and me — a fruit cage full of delicious raspberries and strawberries, into which we would disappear for lengthy gorgings.

Birkhall had another advantage. It was sufficiently far from Balmoral to discourage Queen Mary from suddenly dropping in and catching you improperly dressed or improperly occupied. This was the constant terror of the families nearer the centre of the hive. When Queen Mary came to tea, everything was ship-shape. As is well known she could not be counted on not to open a drawer here or a cupboard there, so all personal paraphernalia had to be extremely carefully concealed.

Birkhall was decorated from floor to ceiling with a valuable collection of Spy cartoons (signed by each victim), which was somewhat overpowering. These had been collected by a previous tenant, the venerable white-bearded courtier, Sir Dighton Probyn, V.C.

This group, taken in 1922, includes Princess Alice, Countess of Athlone (the last surviving grand-daughter of Queen Victoria, who died in 1981 aged ninety-seven), Sir Derek Keppel, the Master of the Household, my mother, Teddy Kennard (my cousin), Gaspard, Mickey Adeane (later Private Secretary to the present Queen), Victoria and Anne Keppel, and Lady May Cambridge (Princess Alice's daughter, now Lady May Abel Smith). Birkhall is today the home of the Queen Mother.

Lord Stamfordham with Sir Harry Lauder, the famous Scottish comedian, still remembered today for such songs as "I Love a Lassie", "Roamin' in the Gloamin'" and "Stop Yer Tickling, Jock". To amuse Sir Harry I was commissioned to play golf with him on the nine hole golf course at Balmoral. They must have been hard up for amusements as it can't have been much fun for him playing with a flapper. I don't remember who won, but neither of us was much good.

Lord Stamfordham was the King's Private Secretary and the most powerful man at court. He had also been Queen Victoria's Private Secretary from 1895 until her death. He was charming, discreet and wise and we all loved him.

Lord Glentanar was considered a great catch as he was very rich. His mother was like a character out of CRANFORD. She selected a bevy of young girls to come and stay at Glen Tanar in Aberdeenshire. But nothing ever came of her schemes (to the chagrin of my mother), which was hardly surprising as we were so heavily chaperoned and never left alone with the "catch" for a single moment. In the end he went off on his own and returned with a foreign bride.

There are interesting faces in this group of 1922. The back row contains Mr. Chichester, Colonel Charteris and Lord Douro (later 5th Duke of Wellington). In the middle row Lady Douro (future Duchess of Wellington and Lady Glentanar's sister), sits next to Princess Andrew of Greece (mother of the Duke of Edinburgh, who would then have been a baby), Captain Bruce, Lady Glentanar, Admiral Farquhar, Charles Carnegie (now Earl of Southesk, who married Edward VII's daughter, Princess Maud), and, on the extreme right, Prince Philip's sisters, Princess Margarita and Princess Theodora. In the front row, with the dog, is Pamela Coventry, then Mrs. Bruce, Mrs. Charteris and Mrs. Adams (another sister of Lady Glentanar) and in front of them Humphrey Walrond, Betty Adams and me.

*B*oating on the Tay where I caught my first salmon. Lady Amy Coats (daughter of the Duke of Richmond), Lady Zia Wernher (daughter of Grand Duke Michael) and Amy's sister-in-law Margaret Coats (later Viscountess Knollys) are all dressed in the latest fashion, Fair Isle sweaters. Sadly, I was unable to follow their example.

*I*n 1922, my mother and I went to stay at Lowther Castle in Westmorland, a huge unmanageable Gothic Castle, built at the beginning of the last century, but set in a beautiful situation on a hill. The terrace was a mile long. The Earl of Lonsdale, known as "The Yellow Earl", was dearly loved in sporting circles. His liveries, cars and carriages were all a deep, butter yellow.

After I was married he would come to Eaton for Chester Races and I danced with him. He always called this "lovely fun". I ensured that he was always served hock and seltzer for breakfast, an eighteenth-century taste he had.

*T*he General Strike of 1926 lasted eleven days. My
mother corralled a lot of my girlfriends to come and
work in the Paddington Station railway men's canteen.
We were set to cleaning up the place, which was by no
means a dainty task. It was black with engrained grime.
By the time we handed it back it was as clean as a
hospital ward. I still have a small silver tray engraved
with my name from the Great Western Railways
thanking me for my labours. The group above shows,
from left to right: Adele Biddulph, Blossom Freeman-
Thomas, myself, my mother. In front of her, Victoria
Keppel, then Miss Rodokanaki. Three (one in front of
the other, from the back): Lady Mildmay, Margaret
Lindsey, Tanis Guinness. Then the other four:
Elizabeth Williamson, Miss Rees, Joan Talbot and
Mary Biddulph. I have to admit that my friends and I
enjoyed the novelty and excitement of the strike and it
was over before it had time to pall.

*M*y mother and I were staying at the British
Embassy in Rome. My mother is on the left. Dick
Molyneux was a courtier who always said he looked
like an elephant, his nose was so long. Beside him is
Lady Sybil Graham, the Ambassadress, and next to
her, Lord Berners, composer, author, painter,
caricaturist and mischief maker.

*T*his photograph of a very young Noël Coward was taken at Reigate Priory, Lord Beatty's home in Surrey. I first met Noël Coward in the house where so many brilliant young men first appeared in our lives, 19 Great Cumberland Place, the home of Beatrice Guinness, the mother of Zita and "Baby" Jungman. We were all thrilled by THE VORTEX when it came out and rushed to see it. Years later I used to stay with him in Jamaica and we lived in houses on the side of a mountain. He was working very hard every day but used to come down from his house for lunch on the terrace with Coley (Cole Lesley) and me. In the evenings we went up there. Noël was kind enough to write the foreword to my memoirs, GRACE AND FAVOUR. He wrote: "I remember her as a gay and attractive girl with dark hair who had the good taste to laugh at my jokes, and the fact that she has never outgrown this agreeable habit has cemented our friendship into such a rock-like consistency that it scarcely wobbled when she asked me to write this foreword." He was fundamentally very nice and kind.

*T*his is the Lido in Venice in 1926, with a lot of smart Italians, foremost amongst them the alarming Princess Jane di San Faustino, holding a black umbrella and dressed as ever like Mary Queen of Scots, unusual beach-wear even sixty years ago. Others are (seated) Ruby Peto and Andrasachi (standing behind) myself and the Duc de Verda. Standing on the right is one of the Robilants.

*T*wo sisters in Venice, Margaret Kahn, now Nin Ryan, a leading New York figure, and her sister Momo Marriott (Maud Marriott, the late wife of General Sir John Marriott). They are the granddaughters of Otto Kahn, a German who became an American, owned a magnificent art collection and financed the Metropolitan Opera House.

*F*ancy dress parties were very much the order of the day. This is the sailors' group at the Robilants' baby party at the Morosoni Palazzo in Venice in 1926. We all went as sailors because that was the cheapest form of fancy dress we could buy in Venice. I am seated fourth from the right, behind the recumbent figure. Second from the right is Zita Jungman.

*Y*ou might think that we look surprisingly gay considering that we are on our way down the salt mines in Austria. Before the war you had to wear that curious costume in order to be allowed down to see the huge beautiful subterranean caves and lakes. The salt mines did not then have the sinister connotation they subsequently acquired. On the first train you see Victor Goodman, Zita Jungman, me, Va Loder and Vera Grenfell.

*T*he younger of the Jungman sisters, called "Baby" when I first knew her, now insists on being called by her Catholic baptismal name, Teresa. The Jungman sisters with Lady Eleanor Smith were leading "Bright Young People". Teresa had a lot of beaux and men in love with her, including Charlie Brocklehurst, Evelyn Waugh and Sunny (the 9th Duke of) Marlborough.

In March 1927 I was staying with Tanis Guinness in Cannes. We went over to Lady Grey's villa on Cap Ferrat with its exquisite garden leading down to the sea. Here at last I made the acquaintance of a much-discussed young man, Stephen Tennant. In my diary I noted: "He is too entrancing to look at, like a delicate Byron – also very intense and amusing." We acted out what I then thought of as a "most improper film, one scene of rape and seduction following the other". I reckoned it would never be passed by the censor! In this line-up are (from left to right) Zita Jungman, Dorothy Wilde (niece of Oscar Wilde), Rex Whistler, Edith Olivier (the Wiltshire author who lived at the Daye House, Wilton), Stephen Tennant, Flora Lion (the portrait painter) and Cecil Beaton. The young men certainly look smarter than the girls.

On the same occasion, we formed a group which we called the Seven-headed God. From the top (left to right) you see Rex Whistler, Stephen Tennant, Captain Crichton, Joan Churston (now Princess Joan Aly Khan), Tanis Guinness, Zita Jungman and me. The photographer was Cecil Beaton, 2 March 1927.

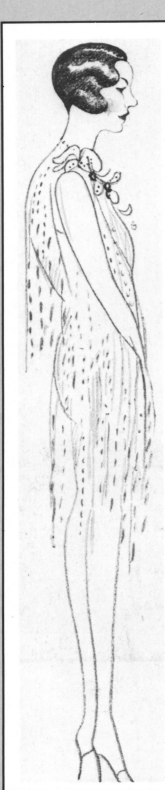

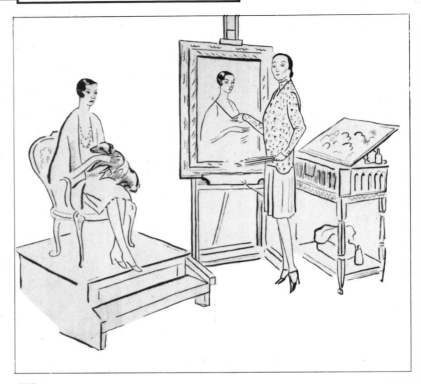

*T*his is one of Cecil Beaton's VOGUE caricatures,
captioned at the time: "Here you see Miss Loelia
Ponsonby, the daughter of the Treasurer to the King,
being painted by the brilliant portrait painter, Flora
Lion. Miss Ponsonby, in red and gold, is having great
difficulty in making her dog keep still" – particularly, I
might add, as I was falling asleep the whole time after
the dissipations of the previous night's party.

*C*ecil Beaton's first work for VOGUE took the form of
caricatures illustrating articles. This one is captioned:
"Miss Loelia Ponsonby, the very attractive daughter of
Sir Frederick Ponsonby, wore a shimmering gown from
Molyneux at the Wilton Ball." The dress was made of
fringe sewn with mother of pearl sequins. I fancied
myself in it a lot. Cecil's powers of observation and
concentration deserve high marks as on the evening of
the ball he was ducked in the Nadder by some of Lord
Herbert's heartier young guests, to the fury of Lady
Pembroke.

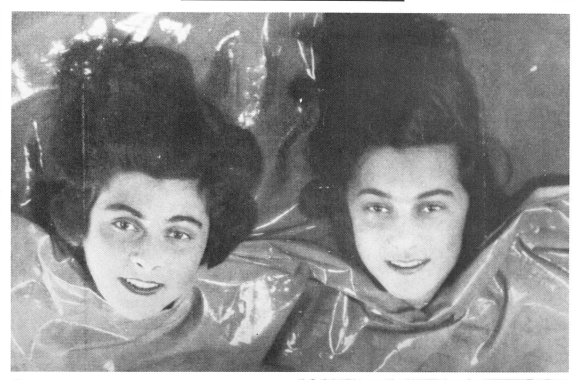

I was one of Cecil Beaton's early sitters. Lili de Alvarez, one of the greatest tennis players of the epoch, drove me to Cecil's parents' house in Sussex Gardens on 15 July 1927. I persuaded her to come in and be photographed too. Cecil made us lie upside down, leaning backwards, our hair entwined and surrounded with lilies that Cecil had pinched from a vase in poor Mrs. Beaton's drawing-room.

Jean Combe (who later married Lord Donegall) and Prince George (later Duke of Kent) photographed on a boat at the seaside.

*T*his picture was taken at the Villa dell' Ombrellino, which hung over Florence from Bellosguardo like a hanging garden of Babylon. It belonged to the famous Mrs. George Keppel, one of the loves of Edward VII's life. I wish I had photographed her. She was the most amusing and I think kindest person I have ever met. Her daughter, Sonia Cubitt, is in the middle of the group. She has amply inherited her mother's wit and generosity of spirit and wrote a book called EDWARDIAN DAUGHTER. On the left is Nancy Tree, then the wife of Ronald Tree, and on the right, Barbara Jenkinson.

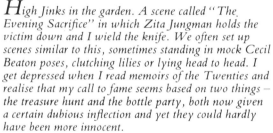

*H*igh Jinks in the garden. A scene called "The Evening Sacrifice" in which Zita Jungman holds the victim down and I wield the knife. We often set up scenes similar to this, sometimes standing in mock Cecil Beaton poses, clutching lilies or lying head to head. I get depressed when I read memoirs of the Twenties and realise that my call to fame seems based on two things – the treasure hunt and the bottle party, both now given a certain dubious inflection and yet they could hardly have been more innocent.

The treasure hunts were thought up by my friends Zita and Teresa Jungman. To start with there were only eight other girls, four couples competing. The clues were very ingenious and Zita was a master of unusual ideas as to where to hide them. For example, once she got the Hovis factory, then on the Thames Embankment, to bake the clue in special loaves. She also persuaded Lord Beaverbrook to print a small edition of the EVENING STANDARD with sham news headlines and a concealed clue.

None of us had much money so we went by bus or underground as speedily as we could. Soon more and more people joined and the hunts got rather out of hand with Rolls Royces jostling each other down mewses and people fighting for the clue. Eventually they were abandoned but taken up by Miss Elsa Maxwell, who claimed in due course to have invented them herself.

The bottle party I have to admit I started. As it now conjures up visions of dingy cellars, drunkenness and police raids I will relate its true origins. My parents were living in a beautiful house on the corner of Marlborough Gate, St. James's Palace. The drawing room had a parquet floor and a piano and seemed all set for a party. One autumn my parents went away for a long shooting week and my brother and I agreed it was the perfect moment to entertain our friends. The snag was that as usual we had no money. I hit on the idea of asking all the girls to bring some food and the young men to bring drink. There was a pretty motley collection laid out on the dining-room table until Michael Arlen, the author of THE GREEN HAT, kindly contributed a dozen bottles of pink champagne. The idea was such a good one and like all good ideas so simple that it caught on and was copied. As we know nearly all young people give bottle parties these days.

A pageant at Dunrobin, the dramatic castle of the Duke of Sutherland. This episode included Bonnie Prince Charlie (me) on the right with Flora Macdonald (Miss Gillan) on the left.

Elizabeth Belloc-Lowndes (later Countess of Iddesleigh), with her sister, Susan (later married to Luiz Marques, owner and editor of the ANGLO-PORTUGUESE NEWS), daughters of the famous Marie Belloc-Lowndes (who wrote over fifty novels), Stephen Tennant and Rex Whistler, whose death in the Second World War was a great sorrow to his many friends. Elizabeth came to Wilsford with a large chicken-skin fan and asked Rex to draw on it. This he did, taking immense pains and care, because one blob would have ruined it completely. I wonder what happened to it. Stephen was very funny and very good-looking. He used to do a marvellous Nijinsky stunt, taking hours dressing up as LE DIEU BLEU. He would come in to take his applause, then pretend to say goodbye for ever, then in a flash return for more applause. It was highly entertaining.

*I*n the spring of 1928 I went on a Mediterranean cruise with the Beattys in their yacht, the SHEELAH. Our first stop was Malta where we spent a month or so happily moored in a creek with no seasickness worries. Lord Beatty's son, David, was serving in the flagship of Sir Roger Keyes, Commander-in-Chief of the Mediterranean Fleet. The two Admirals (Sir Roger on the left and Lord Beatty on the right) were both heroes of World War One. They had been friends for years; in fact they were both in the Boxer Rising in China in 1900.

*T*his is a dreadful picture of Edwina Mountbatten, who was a most beautiful glamorous creature. I am on her left. On the right, with an umbrella, stands Lord Beatty.

BALMORAL CASTLE

PROGRAMME

CHARLIE CHAPLIN

in

"THE CIRCUS"

Written, Directed and Produced by *CHARLIE CHAPLIN*

━

And Incidents from

"THE TROOPING OF THE COLOUR"
"MODES AND MANNERS AT THE ZOO"
Selection by "THE SQUIRE OCTETTE"

by

BRITISH TALKING PICTURES LIMITED.

*As presented before Their Majesties The King and Queen
on Wednesday, 19th September, 1928.*

*W*e were often included in the Balmoral fun. A memorable night was a showing of Charlie Chaplin's latest film on 19 September 1928 in the presence of King George V and Queen Mary. This was a great event as it was almost unknown to fix a projector and screen in a private house. Unfortunately we started too late from Birkhall. When we arrived at Balmoral we were ushered into a totally silent room with the audience seated in glum rows staring at an empty screen. In the front row Their Majesties sat, silent and forbidding, with the other members of the Royal Family. The most extraordinary part of this tale is that when some kindly character asked if we had had a puncture or breakdown (more than likely in our rickety old car), my parents failed to catch at this miraculous straw. The straw was airily dismissed and the truth told – we were late in leaving. It was a strange lapse for a normally resourceful courtier.

*M*yself as my ancestress, Lady Bessborough. Cecil Beaton was dressed as Gainsborough and his two sisters as the artist's daughters. We were always dressing up in the name of charity. Our performances were too pathetically amateur for words and it is a wonder that the audiences stood it.

In my memoirs I captioned this photograph of me by Cecil Beaton appropriately enough as "Fine feathers make fine birds" – the Westminster Tiara was subsequently sold to America and the famous pair of perfectly matched Arcot diamonds split up.

*M*y wedding to Bendor took place on the morning of
20 February 1930, in the Registry Office off
Buckingham Palace Road. A special but rather dreary
room had been set aside for us and hastily decorated
with tapestries, flowers and Chippendale chairs from
Bourdon House, Bendor's London home. My wedding
outfit was not a success. In desperation I pinned to it
two large purple orchids sent from Bendor that morning.
To celebrate his wedding Bendor had given his tenants a
week's free rent and cancelled all arrears. At a time of
unemployment and trade depression this was a popular
gesture and people swarmed round the Registry Office
to give him a cheer. I had been so strictly brought up
never to have any publicity, that I was quite
unprepared for the crowds that turned up, and darted
into the car like a scalded cat, leaving my bridegroom
to acknowledge the cheers alone.

*T*he best man was Winston Churchill, even in those
days an awe-inspiring figure, though none of us realised
the great heights he would eventually attain.

The Gentlemen of the Press with hats and extraordinarily old-fashioned-looking cameras, like joke characters in a Hollywood movie of the date.

Here are two wedding guests arriving. Poppy Thursby and Catherine Carnarvon who were old friends.

*A*ppropriately we boarded the CUTTY SARK from the Westminster steps and then waited for our guests to arrive. On the extreme left is Sacherevell Sitwell, a very old friend who was also present when in 1969 I married Martin Lindsay.

*T*he Westminsters at sea.

*E*aton, the official home of the Westminsters, was more like a village than a country house. I was often asked if it was the largest house in England. The reply was that at Wentworth Woodhouse, Lord Fitzwilliam's house in Yorkshire, they could put up two more guests than our maximum of sixty. The clock tower which stood 178 feet high was modelled on Big Ben. During the Second World War the house was commandeered by the War Office and handed back in a dreadful state in 1960. It was demolished and all that remain today are the clock tower and the Chapel and some stables.

I loved it dearly and in my imagination the old Eaton is still there.

*T*his passage led from the small wing in which we lived, to the main house where we entertained vast parties but at other times hardly ever went into.

The main staircase in the big house. The knights in armour had pale chamois leather bottoms sticking out. I thought they looked rather indecent, so I had them discreetly covered in old red velvet.

My sitting-room was the most successful of all the rooms I decorated. On the walls loose, willow-green silk-damask hung in gentle folds above the pine skirting board. At one end a French armorial tapestry just fitted above a green velvet sofa. The carpet was a bronze-toned Aubusson, and the same colours were picked up in a painted Spanish leather screen, the greens and red-browns complementing each other perfectly. Between the windows was a magnificent pair of Chinoiserie laquer cupboards and in the bay was a Carlton House writing-table, surmounted by a gilt gallery. A Waterford glass chandelier glittered overhead, and the final touch was the enchanting Hogarth which we hung above the mantelpiece. Bendor kindly allowed me to plunder the big house of all the most beautiful things I wanted. The flowers were always perfect.

*T*he wing in which we lived, set at right angles to the main house. There the dining-room seated only a dozen people so was quite snug after the other two large ones in the main house.

*M*y bedroom had three windows and looked down the terrace. Leading off it was a big bathroom. The bath was surrounded in fawn-coloured marble and the water spouted through a lion's mouth. On the opposite side a jib door opened into a large dressing-room, round which were built-in cupboards lined with rose-sprigged chintz, and fitted with shelves and racks and pegs and rails.

The bedroom itself was panelled in Queen Anne style and painted pale fawn. On the bed was a wonderfully well-preserved Queen Anne bedspread with an intricate design of exotic flowers with verdigris green leaves scattered over a fine silk damask ground. I had the luck to find some velvet of the same virulent acid green as the leaves, which I had made into curtains and bed-back, and I slept between pale pink crêpe de chine sheets, ornamented with applique designs in satin.

*B*endor had many homes. I think he was happiest at Lochmore, a typical Scotch mansion on the west coast of Inverness-shire. I thought it one of the most beautiful spots on this earth, looking out, as it did, from a small rise in the garden over the wild beauty beyond. Here Bendor loved to fish and I loved to garden. I became quite a good salmon fisher too.

*M*imizan was a remote house in the Landes between Bordeaux and Biarritz which Bendor built before the First World War for boar-hunting. It was designed by the South African architect, Herbert Baker. The house was situated in pine trees on the edge of a huge lake. There was no road by which to approach it and so visitors could only reach it by means of a speedboat sent to fetch them from the far side of the lake. Now the whole area has been commercialised and hideous little bungalows have sprung up everywhere. Only the doorway seen in the photograph remains.

*K*ylestrome was another house on the Westminster Scotch estate. We used to take a ferry across the narrow entrance to the huge inlet, which formed a natural harbour. Now I believe there is a bridge. The CUTTY SARK was very often moored in this lake where there was a waterfall which conveniently recharged all the batteries on board. During the war many ships used to hide there.

*W*orld's End. This romantic little house, not far from Llangollen, could be discovered by going up a winding lane. It was very solitary in those days and the local gossip was that Queen Elizabeth I had gone there to have a baby. I forget if a father was named!

Now it is a nature trail I believe, so the mysterious solitude may have gone. We used it for large shooting lunches sent out from Eaton.

*H*ere I stand before the ornamental doorway by which the cabins were reached on the FLYING CLOUD. It was designed by Detmar Blow to resemble the front door of a Cotswold house, with its big concave shell above it carved out of old seasoned oak.

*B*endor had two yachts, a steam yacht called the CUTTY SARK and the FLYING CLOUD, a sailing ship.

I dreaded every minute spent on board knowing full well that I was the envy of all, except other sea-sick sufferers like myself. What a waste of those floating palaces it was. They complemented each other in style by being totally dissimilar. I don't know which I hated the more.

The more romantic was certainly the FLYING CLOUD. She was a dream boat (as long as she remained in harbour). To be technical she was an auxiliary twin-screw masted shooner, built in 1927. She was 203.5 feet long and her gross tonnage was 1,178.74. At the time she was one of the thirty largest yachts in the world with a crew of forty men. Every cabin, saloon and staircase was in pale, unvarnished oak, all the furniture was Queen Anne and in perfect scale, which must have been very hard to find. She was an ultra-luxurious Peter Pan pirate ship. The trouble with her, from my point of view, was that she crawled along, rolling, pitching and wallowing and taking an eternity to get from one point to the next. Rarely was the wind right for the sails to be set, but on those odd occasions she was certainly a wonderful sight. Most of the time we had to trust a rather feeble auxiliary. On some days we made no headway at all while I lay groaning on my heaving couch. I was however very lucky to see the beautiful Adriatic in the days before tourists.

The CUTTY SARK was a very different kettle of fish. Her origins were rather romantic. At the end of the First World War, Major Keswick of the China trading firm of Jardine, Matheson and Co. took over the hull of a half-built destroyer and completed her as a yacht. In due course Bendor bought her and had her transformed into a luxury yacht. This of course happened long before my time.

The one good thing about the CUTTY SARK was her speed and reliability. She could always be relied upon to keep good time. Thus I could keep my eye on the clock and know when my misery was likely to end. This was more than counterbalanced by the disadvantages of the destroyer which rolled and pitched to the very limit of safety. My cabin was very large and situated in the stern of the ship, a most unsalubrious spot as her antics were more frisky there than anywhere on board. Once we were in St. Jean de Luz harbour when Winston and Clemmie Churchill, who were staying in Biarritz, came on board with the idea of making a trip to Spain. During lunch (at which we had blackcurrant tart) I heard the groaning and squeaking beginning, which was always a Cassandra sound for me. When we went on deck there was no doubt that a storm was brewing and, quick as a flash, Winston announced that he had some very important political papers to attend to. He and his wife ripped down the companionway and were soon on the safety of the shore.

As usual I had to listen to all the fantasies handed out to reassure the land lubber:
"It may be blowing here, but once we're round the point, it will be as flat as a lake."
"Sea-sick, don't be so ridiculous. Nobody could possibly be. . . ."

Another horror for the sufferer was the kind of remedy served to the luckless victim – pills of all colours and shapes, champagne or stout or a mixture of both. There was no end to the horrors that laid briefly on my violently-reacting tummy.

*B*endor standing with a fine seven-foot-high gigantum
lily which I had planted at Lochmore.

*B*endor on the steps at Mimizan.

*T*his was my boar-hunting costume. The hat was very becoming, the brim was banded in gold braid and the crown edged with black ostrich feathers. I am wearing the gilt hunt buttons.

I entitled this picture "Studies in expression of our eminent poet – Mr. Sitwell". Sachie Sitwell.

I suppose it is not often that one sees a Duke disguised as a cabaret star. We posed for this in Barcelona. From left to right Georgia Sitwell, me, Bendor, and Sacheverell Sitwell.

On the same occasion Zita Jungman, Georgia and Sacheverell Sitwell "go for a ride".

*O*ur first public appearance was at the Grand
National at Aintree, and in fact it was my first visit to
the racecourse.

A tennis party at Eaton. From left to right: Professor Lindemann (later Lord Cherwell), the celebrated scientist who became a Cabinet Minister (it was he who shared Churchill's alarm at our country's lack of defences against the mounting aggression of Germany in the 1930s); Joan Marjoribanks (who married Michael Duff briefly); Enid Raphael (a friend from "Bright Young People" days whom I invited rather bravely in spite of Bendor's anti-Semitic prejudice – sadly, she committed suicide quite young). And Count Paul Munster at whose house in Austria the Duke of Windsor stayed for a while after the abdication and before his marriage.

Tommy Graves and Gladys, Lady Delamere, of WHITE MISCHIEF fame.

*G*eorgia Sitwell on a camel in Egypt during our visit there in 1931. One of the excitements of our journey was to be shown over the tomb of Tutankhamun by Howard Carter, who was still working in a cave next to the site of his great discovery.

*H*igh jinks on board with Eddie Compton of Newby Hall. The Flying Cloud *was such a large yacht that there always seemed to be endless opportunities for fun and games.*

*M*ore high jinks on board the FLYING CLOUD.

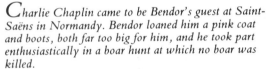

*C*harlie Chaplin came to be Bendor's guest at Saint-Saëns in Normandy. Bendor loaned him a pink coat and boots, both far too big for him, and he took part enthusiastically in a boar hunt at which no boar was killed.

*R*andolph Churchill with me in France at one of Bendor's boar-hunts. He was one of our frequent visitors. Nobody who did not see him when he was young could possibly appreciate how gloriously good-looking he was.

*B*endor shooting at World's End, watched enthusiastically by his loader, 1933. He was a very good shot.

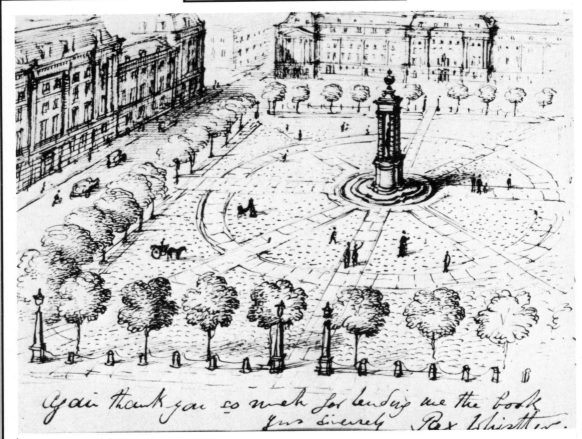

Again thank you so much for lending me the book. Yrs sincerely Rex Whistler.

Rex Whistler was generous with his drawings. This is one he sent to Bendor. In those days Grosvenor Square had high railings and a thick hedge. There was an idea of clearing them away after the war. This is Rex's idea of how the Square might have looked. When I married, Rex designed me a book-plate which was a view of St. James's Palace within a roccoco frame.

Sacheverell and Georgia Sitwell. In those days the Sitwells (Edith, Osbert and Sacheverell) were utterly unlike anybody else. They held a unique position in the arts. Today I suppose the nearest equivalent would be some very elevated, cultural pop-star, but they excited far more awe than any pop-star. They were extraordinarily clever and funny and there were three of them which made them still more disconcerting.

*O*ne of my rare public appearances as Duchess of Westminster because Bendor so disapproved of anybody playing "the Lady Bountiful". I am seated with the Mayor and Corporation of Chester.

*C*lemmie Churchill at Eaton. A good, keen tennis player.

A shooting party. From left to right: Hazel Clowes, Prince Arthur of Connaught, Bendor, George Thursby, Eddie Compton, my mother, Princess Arthur of Connaught, Sylvia Compton and Evan Charteris (the author and barrister).

Me reading in a charming chair at Mimizan.

A little weekend party at Eaton: from left to right (standing) Nicole Hornby, Ikey Bell (the famous huntsman and hound breeder), Esme Reiss, John Pole-Carew, Gladys Cooper (famous first as Gaiety Girl and later as an actress, then married to Neville Pearson), Georgia Sitwell, Helen Fitzgerald, Sheila Milbanke, Poppy Thursby, Bridget Parsons, me, Bridget Poulett, Marguerite Bernadotte, Colin Buist, Anthony Knebworth (who died in a flying accident before the war), and Bendor.

Seated: Michael Duff, Neville Pearson, Michael Hornby, Sachie Sitwell, Chips Channon, Seymour Berry (now Lord Camrose), Lord Poulett and Charles Reiss.

*M*y father and mother at Mimizan. My father was recuperating at the time with a broken collar bone.

Bendor and his favourite dachshund, Mr. Dempsey.

This conversation piece shows me and Colonel Lloyd (known as "Lloydo"). The dear old boy had taken part in the Jameson raid in December 1895.

*M*yself painting on silk in the drawing-room at Lochmore.

*I*n bed at Lochmore in 1934. Behind me, the coat of arms shows the arms of the Grosvenors halved with the arms of the Ponsonbys.

"*The Birdikins*", a nickname for the Churchills, borrowed from PUNCH. I think they personified a very devoted couple. Once at Eaton, Bendor had a famous conjuror staying, who could empty your pockets and remove your wristwatch without your knowing. The conjuror took Winston's braces off and he was so furious that he retired upstairs in high dudgeon and threatened to leave.

A domestic scene. I embroider as Bendor dozes peacefully by the fire.

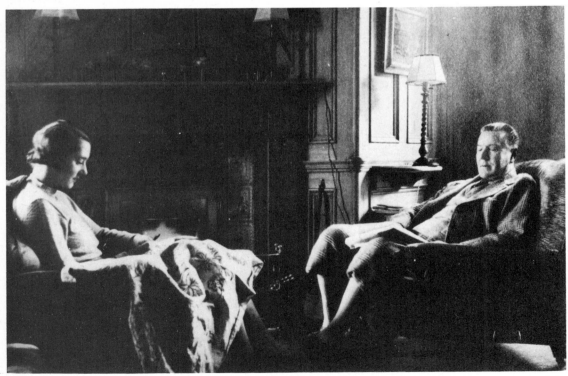

Bendor and me with our favourite dogs.

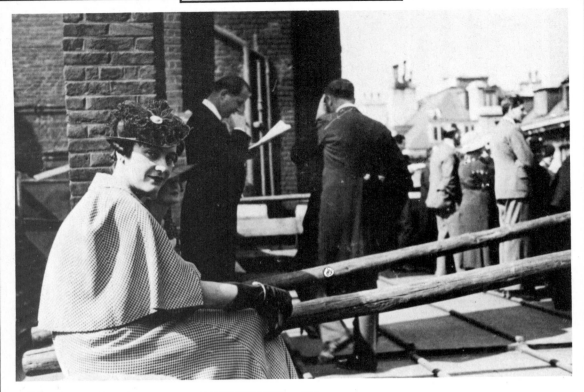

The Silver Jubilee of King George V was celebrated in 1935, a few months before my father's death. I watched the procession from the roof of my parents' house in St. James's Palace.

The Thanksgiving Service took place on 6 May 1935 on a hot summer's day. Several carriage processions made their way to St. Paul's Cathedral, where the Archbishop of Canterbury gave an address. My father was in the procession.

*T*he christening of Francis Sitwell, second son of
Sachie and Georgia. I am his godmother. From left to
right: Jimmy Foster (cousin of Lord Berners and owner
of Apley Park, Salop), myself, Georgia with Francis,
Sachie with Reresby. Francis was born in September
1935.

*C*hips Channon and his wife Honor (daughter of the
head of the Guinness family, the Earl of Iveagh).
Chips was a famous host, M.P. and diarist. He was a
great life-enhancer and extremely kind.

*P*aul Maze painting in Molly Buccleuch's garden. Paul Maze met Winston Churchill in the trenches in the First World War. He and Winston painted together. It was often said that he taught Winston how to paint but he used to say: "Maybe some of his paintings had a little touch of me in them." On this occasion I sat for him all afternoon under a tree. At least I thought I was sitting for him. When finally I said I must have a look, I found he had only painted the tree.

A group in a wagonette at Faringdon in 1936. Faringdon was a notably eccentric house owned by Lord Berners, where to this day the doves are dyed pink. On open days members of the public have been known to enquire how doves are bred that colour. On horseback is the present owner, Robert Heber-Percy. In the wagonette are Penelope Betjeman (wife of the Poet Laureate), Xandra Haig (who later married the historian, Lord Dacre), Lord Berners and Aldous Huxley.

A shooting party at Wilton. In the back row (from left to right), Nell Stavordale (later Lady Ilchester), Mary Herbert (later Lady Pembroke), Bee Pembroke (Mary Herbert's mother-in-law), Liz Paget (later Hofmannsthal), David Herbert and me. In the front: Tortor Gilmour (one of the four daughters of Lord Chelsea, known as "the Cadogan Square"), Marjorie Anglesey (sister of Diana Cooper) and the Duchess of York.

A group at Wilton in December 1936, shortly before the Abdication. From left to right Sidney Herbert (the heir), Malcolm Bullock (the Conservative M.P.), the Duchess of York (now the Queen Mother), Tony Herbert, David Herbert, Mary Herbert (Sidney's wife), the Duke of York (later George VI) and the Duke of Alba. We had no idea of the drama that was about to burst on the world but I remember Lady Pembroke saying she thought the Duchess of York very depressed.

*T*he Duchess of Buccleuch entertained a large weekend party at Boughton for the Duke and Duchess of Kent. Myself with the Duchess.

*S*em, a funny little monkey of a man who was a famous French caricaturist. He was a friend of Proust and one night Proust took him for a taxi ride from Trouville to Cabourg. Every time they turned a corner they encountered a stray cow which looked set to charge the car. Sem said to Proust: "You invite me for a ride and then you expect me to take part in a bullfight in the heart of the pampas!"

A new hobby, which was fashionable for a time – bicycles on skis. Eustace Long is followed by Sallie Monkland who later that year married my brother. I follow. This picture was taken in St. Moritz in 1936.

These were the robes I wore for the Coronation of George VI in 1937. The robes had to be worn over the usual full court dress. The Earl Marshal issued precise orders concerning the robes. For a Duchess the robe or mantle had to be "of crimson velvet, the cape thereof to be furred with miniver pure and powdered with four rows of ermine, the edging five inches in breadth, the train two yards", the coronet "a circle with eight strawberry leaves, all of equal height". The caps of the coronets were to be of crimson velvet, turned up with ermine with a gold tassel on the top. It was very difficult to put the coronet on the moment when the Queen was crowned because it had to be fitted behind the tiara.

After the ceremony at Westminster Abbey I spotted the Mountbattens slipping out by a side door and wisely followed them. I had been invited to lunch at the House of Lords but fortunately decided to go instead to Brendan Bracken's house to play bridge with Duff Cooper and many others. We had a delicious lunch of lobster and asparagus still in our robes and tiaras. Meanwhile the guests at the House of Lords had a terrible time, unable to get food or to escape. These photographs were taken later in the day at Great Tangley Manor, by then my brother's house.

Maxine Elliott, the famous Edwardian actress and hostess to royalty and politicians, at her villa, the Château de l'Horizon, at Golfe-Juan, near Cannes, 1937 (it now belongs to the Aga Khan). Nobody seems to have a good word for great hostesses. The people invited to their salons make amusing but bitter in-jokes while those not invited averred vehemently that they would never deign to go if they were. Much is heard about such figures as Lady Cunard, Lady Colefax and Lady Ottoline Morrell, but less well-known today is Maxine Elliott. She and her sister came from Maine in America. Gertrude married a very famous actor, Sir Johnston Forbes-Robertson. (I was very keen on him as he said I had a voice like liquid pearls.) Maxine must have been very beautiful when young. She had the largest eyes I have ever seen and the pupils did seem to be made of black velvet. By the time I knew her she had got very fat which was unfortunate as she had tiny little Madame Butterfly feet that had quite a job supporting her considerable weight. Maxine had a monkey at the villa called Kiki. His position in the house was of supreme importance. If he bit a guest, no sympathy was extended. Maxine simply ordered her butler to bring the iodine. Maxine died in 1940.

The next three pictures were taken during a visit to her villa in 1937.

Maxine's villa, the Château de l'Horizon, was between the railway and the sea on a narrow strip of land and on rocks high above the sea. Friends complained that there was no beach and that it was impossible to swim from the rocks. Maxine built a swimming-pool on the rocks and from it a water-chute down which you glided into the sea. Here the author, Beverley Nichols, prepares to go down the chute.

Rex Harrison and Edythe Baker, sitting on the terrace of Maxine's villa. Rex Harrison had recently been playing in FRENCH WITHOUT TEARS *at the Criterion. Edythe Baker was a brilliant pianist and a girl friend of the Duke of Kent before his marriage to Princess Marina.*

Another of Maxine's guests, Nada Milford Haven, sister-in-law of Lord Mountbatten and a daughter of Grand Duke Michael of Russia. The Grand Duke lived at the Villa Kazbeck at Cannes and laid the foundation stones of the Casino and Carlton Hotel at Cannes. Nada's son was Prince Philip's best man when he married the Queen.

*W*hen I first went to America in 1937 with my great friends Flash and Myrtle Kellett, we had the most glorious time enjoying the unceasing hospitality of American friends. In those days it was unheard-of for the English to repay their generous American hosts in any way whatever, a feeble "Look us up if you come over" being the best invitation the Americans got. But we decided to give a ball at the end of our stay, just before Christmas. With the help of Cecil Beaton (who drew the caricatures) we decorated the flower niches of New York's new hotel, Hampshire House, with cutout models of well-known New York figures, the old guard as well as the new. The party was a sensation and the guests danced frantically to the latest dance "the Big Apple". Here the real-life figures of Cecil, myself, Myrtle and Flash Kellett (who was an M.P.) can be seen in front of cut-outs of the English contingent (front row), (and behind) the Duke and Duchess of Marlborough, and Cecil.

A further bevy of characters – this time of fashionable Americans. Front row: Gloria Baker, Elsa Maxwell and Cholly Knickerbocker. Back row: Ali Mackintosh, Will Stewart, Condé Nast and Serge Obolensky.

*T*he El Morocco had become the most famous
nightclub in Manhattan in 1937. The banquettes were
upholstered in zebra stripes of midnight blue and white
(not plastic as they would be today). For Hollywood
stars it was "a required pit-stop" and many Europeans
made it their first port of call after disembarking at Pier
90. I am seated with Charlie Payson (father of Sandra
Weidenfeld).

A somewhat humorous portrait of the late Duke of
Marlborough.

*A*lice von Hofmannsthal, who looked like a beautiful Persian miniature. She was the sister of Vincent Astor, one of the richest men in America. She was first married to Prince Serge Obolensky as his second wife and then to Raimund von Hofmannsthal, son of the famous poet Hugo van Hofmannsthal, who collaborated with Richard Strauss, writing libretti for famous operas such as DER ROSENKAVALIER and ARABELLA. Later she married twice more. With her is her daughter, Romana.

*B*ill Paley, Tom Mitford and Caroline Paget at Kammer. Bill Paley, now head of CBS in America, dressed (as all the English and Americans seemed to be at that time) in elaborate Austrian costume. Tom Mitford, the only son of Lord Redesdale and brother of the famous Mitford sisters. He died of wounds in Burma in 1945. Caroline Paget, daughter of the Angleseys, was said to be the most attractive girl of her generation. She married Sir Michael Duff.

*T*om Mitford stands between Tilly Losch (left) and Bill Paley's then wife, Dorothy. Tilly Losch, the Viennese dancer, was first married to Edward James (the eccentric millionaire and art collector who lives in Mexico and builds extraordinary follies in the jungle) and then in the war to Lord Carnarvon.

*K*ätchen Kommer with me at Kammer. Kätchen was an extraordinary person and a great character in our lives. He fancied himself as a marriage broker, but I don't think he brought off many successes. This was just as well as he said he would always claim the firstborn child. He would have gathered a strange menagerie.

Mr. and Mrs. Averell Harriman with Raimund von Hofmannsthal at Kammer. Averell Harriman is now married to Pam Churchill, Randolph's first wife.

Iris Tree, the Bohemian daughter of actor-manager Sir Herbert Beerbohm Tree, at Kammer in 1938. She was then married to the giant actor, Friedrich Ledebur. She played the nun in THE MIRACLE. One night we were all taken to a barbecue party further down the lake. When Iris had had enough, she simply stepped into the lake fully clothed and swam back to Schloss Kammer. I longed to copy her.

Kammer was an extraordinary castle on a promontory of Lake Attersee. It was built round a courtyard with several families living in various ramifications of it. Everybody was supposed to be friends, but there were tremendous feuds and tensions. People who seemed friendly one day cut each other the next. I was conventional, spoke no German and was permanently amazed at what was going on.

High jinks once more. This time Flash Kellett embellishes the statuary at Lady Desborough's house, Taplow.

Drogo Montagu waterskiing at Karinder Hutte in Austria. This was a new thrill in the thirties. Drogo was the son of Lord Sandwich and the first husband of my friend Tanis Phillips.

I first went to Hollywood before the war and visited a film studio where I met the famous star, Errol Flynn.

Compton Beauchamp, a lovely moated house, which was half Queen Anne and half Georgian, under the downs near Shrivenham, Berkshire. I took it for a year in 1935.

*D*uff Cooper playing with Caroline Child-Villiers at Sutton Courtenay.

*E*velyn Waugh, Lady Juliet Duff, Malcolm Bullock, Evelyn's second wife, Laura, and Betty Cranborne (later Lady Salisbury).

*P*rincess Joan Aly Khan at Ascot, 1938. She is the mother of the Aga Khan, and was first married to the multi-millionaire, Loel Guinness.

A group at Faringdon. From left to right Carol Radowitz (unknown), Gerald Berners, Constant Lambert the composer, Veronica and Edward Tennant with Teresa Jungman between them.

*C*annes *1938. When staying with Maxine Elliott, it was the custom most evenings to repair to the terrace of the Carlton Hotel for cocktails. At the next table we found Foxy Gwynne (later Lady Sefton) and the Duke and Duchess of Windsor, the latter looking somewhat forceful. The Windsors were then living at the Château de la Croe on Cap d'Antibes.*

*C*ecil Beaton at Maxine Elliott's villa in 1938.*

The Windsors at Cannes on another occasion. The Duchess, Foxy Gwynne, Lord Sefton, Lady Brownlow and the Duke. It was Kitty Brownlow's husband, Perry, who had accompanied Mrs. Simpson on her dramatic journey to the South of France just before the Abdication.

My brother, who had the romantic name of Gaspard. As a child he was of the cherubic type much favoured by grown-ups. Any favouritism going went to this golden haired boy-angel rather than to me, who was plain, sallow and suppressed. Our characters were very different. He was courageous, enjoyed skiing and mountaineering and was an optimist. He was perfectly happy amongst the cheerful extroverts in White's Club, while I have always felt more at home with complex characters. He won the DSO in the 1940 retreat.

Throughout the war, Ronald Tree, a rich Anglophile American, offered his Oxfordshire house, Ditchley, for Winston Churchill to escape to when London became too much of a strain or "when the moon was high" and Chequers therefore too conspicuous a target for German bombers. The Prime Minister took full advantage of this generous offer. This is a group on the steps of the house. The back four are Malcolm Bullock, Pricilla Bullock, John Erne, and Anthony Eden (then Foreign Secretary). The next two are Davina Erne and Mogs Gage. The front six are Nancy Tree, Clemmie Churchill, me and Professor Lindemann. Behind me sits Beatrice Eden (Anthony Eden's first wife).

Sutton Courtenay near Abingdon, Berkshire. The house belonged to Norah Lindsay, a famous garden-designer. She was a friend of the Souls and Diana Cooper's aunt. I rented this house for a summer before the war.

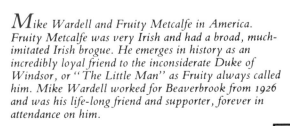

A game of croquet at Sutton Courtenay. Flash Kellett plays, while Porchie Carnarvon and Myrtle Kellett wait, and four shadows watch the proceedings.

*M*ike Wardell and Fruity Metcalfe in America. Fruity Metcalfe was very Irish and had a broad, much-imitated Irish brogue. He emerges in history as an incredibly loyal friend to the inconsiderate Duke of Windsor, or ''The Little Man'' as Fruity always called him. Mike Wardell worked for Beaverbrook from 1926 and was his life-long friend and supporter, forever in attendance on him.

A group at Boughton, the Northamptonshire seat of the Duke of Buccleuch. From left to right: Mrs. Gerard Leigh, Michael and Nicole Hornby, Gerard Leigh, Bill Astor, Molly Buccleuch, Laura Corrigan, Colin Davidson, Xandra Haig and Walter Buccleuch.

*C*harlie Londonderry. Amongst other political appointments, Lord Londonderry held the post of Lord Privy Seal. His wife was famous for her eve-of-session parties at Londonderry House in Park Lane. Sir Richard Sykes, owner of Sledmere, a famous stud in Yorkshire, and Adele Cavendish, better known as Adele Astaire, Fred Astaire's sister.

Staying with the Sitwells at Weston Hall, near Towcester, for Christmas in 1939. I always took a small sack of coal with me when I went to stay during the war, because there was not much fuel around and it was so cold. However, this time it was Christmas and a good fire was blazing in the grate. The Greek photographer, Costa, recorded the scene as I did my embroidery sitting opposite Georgia and Sachie. The photograph was published in the SKETCH and William Joyce, the infamous Lord Haw-Haw, got hold of it and referred to it in one of his "Germany calling" broadcasts. His message was that this was how the English upper class bore the sufferings of war while the lower orders were out fighting. "This," he said, "is the sort of scene you are fighting for."

Tommy MacDougal with the old Berkshire hounds.

Anthony Eden with Mogs Gage (Lord Gage's first wife, the daughter of Lord Desborough) at Ditchley Park.

My portrait, done with a palette knife by Palestrelli.

A portrait of me by Cannons of Hollywood.

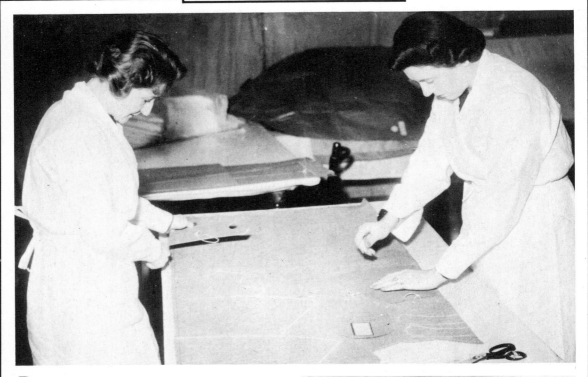

*D*uring the war one of my activities was to make hospital clothing. One of the jobs was to cut out layers of flannel shirts with an electric cutter, very conscious that one slip of the hand could ruin fifty yards of flannel in a second.

*T*his picture by the famous American photographer, Louise Dahl-Wolfe, was entitled "The only Duchess Box-Holder at Covent Garden". The caption went on: "The Duchess of Westminster is a member of the General Committee of the 'Break the News' Film Premiere being organised by the Duchess of Buccleuch and Queensberry in aid of the Y.W.C.A. Central Club and the London Y.W.C.A. at the Cambridge Theatre on May 19, which H.R.H. the Duchess of Kent has promised to attend. The Duchess of Westminster is the only duchess whose name appears on the Covent Garden subscribers list as a box-holder, although other Duchesses, including their Graces of Buccleuch, Rutland and Marlborough, are regular opera-goers."

*F*rom left to right: Lord Alfred Douglas, Duff Cooper, Kathleen (Lady) Queensberry, Ed Stanley (Lord Stanley of Alderley), Diana Cooper, Anne Mappin and Francis (Lord) Queensberry. I did not know Lord Alfred Douglas but, in January 1941, I told my friend Francis Queensberry how interested I would be to meet him. He said nothing would be easier than to get his uncle down for the weekend. So I chose a carefully-selected party including Duff and Diana, and instructed them that no one was to mention Oscar Wilde on the first day. "You, Duff, will bring it up, perhaps after lunch tomorrow." But hardly was Alfred Douglas in the hall before he began talking about Oscar and we heard nothing else the entire weekend. Unfortunately the old scamp lied like a trooper and said that he was not Oscar's boyfriend. Then, a few months later when he next needed the money, he sold his whole story. But he was not unattractive. You could see the ravages of good looks.

On Monday morning when this strange weekend was over, Diana came into my room and said, "I'm sure the old sod hasn't enjoyed himself so much since Oscar died."

*I*an Fleming, the creator of James Bond, on the beach at Cannes.

At the beginning of the war I moved into a charming Georgian House in Surrey, called Send Grove. It suited me perfectly and I felt that the house and I were made for each other. I thought the house small enough to manage, but in time it proved beyond my means and I moved into a smaller house, the nearby cottage, called the Old Vicarage, where I still live today.

Send Grove was once used as an inspiration in the strip cartoon, "Carol Day".

High jinks in a rubbish heap. I sit in an upturned car.

An unusual picture of a press lord – Esmond Rothermere in a rubbish heap. He was Chairman of Associated Newspapers and the DAILY MAIL. His wife Ann later married Ian Fleming.

*A*nn Fleming returning from a trip snorkling at Goldeneye.

*I*an and Ann Fleming in Jamaica.
Ian Fleming was a curious and complex person, and immensely attractive to women. Had his nose not been broken in a boxing match at school, he would have been very good-looking. He was both clever and conceited. He delighted in giving advice on every topic imaginable and it was not always good. I can cite two examples of this. At a time when he was working in Naval Intelligence, he wrote me a letter along the Beaverbrook lines: "There will be no war." As he had access to much secret information I of course believed him. Then, in the first post-war election in 1945, Ian was convinced the Conservatives would win. I was of another opinion, and a heated argument took place at a dinner party, during which Ian covered me with withering scorn. Finally he asked if I would bet on the result. He suggested "What about a pound majorities?" and I agreed without appreciating quite what that implied. Labour swept in with a majority of 186. Ian grumbled that the worst part of this painful result was having to pay me my winnings. He later admitted he had been to Central Office to confer with top brass on the day when he made the bet, so he thought he was betting on a certainty, which I thought was rather hot stuff.

So much has been written about Ian by people who did not know him but I knew him well and one of my claims to fame is that he gave me the manuscript of his first novel CASINO ROYALE to read. I came to a slightly indelicate sexy passage and I reminded him that Lord Kemsley was very straitlaced and he might well lose his job on Kemsley Newspapers. Ian listened to these foolish words and removed the passage. It is funny to think of that now, but anyway he made up for it later.

Ann Fleming at Goldeneye.

I went to stay with Ian in Jamaica several times. While serving in Intelligence with Sir William Stephenson (better known as "Intrepid"), Ian hired a boat and went round the island, searching for a completely private beach where he could build a house. Having found the perfect site, he built his own personal style of house. To start with it was strangely uncomfortable with no windows or shutters, just large square holes in the wall, so that the view could be enjoyed unimpeded by what Americans call "drapes". In daytime this was fine, but at night, when the lamps were lit, every insect known to man seemed to pour in from the darkness outside. Some were vast, some minute, but all were abhorrent to me as I have a particular dislike of insects. Neither Ian nor Ann paid any attention to my cries and all I could do was to sit cringing in a corner.

One day Ian said to me, "Lil" – he always called me that as Loelia is meant to be Russian for Lily – "You go constantly to America, why don't you find me a rich tenant for this house next winter?"

I replied: "It isn't a starter. It hasn't got a bathroom and no American would consider that."

"True," he said, "but what's wrong with the sea?"

My words must have sunk in as the following year he greeted me with the news that, owing to my demands for extreme luxury, he had installed a bathroom. I envisaged wallowing in glorious hot water, only to find that there was but one cold tap. I had to bribe Violet, the Jamaican maid, to bring me a kettle of hot water. Not surprisingly, the hoped-for American never materialised to rent Goldeneye in my day.

I cannot say I enjoyed my Goldeneye days as I soon discovered that the reason I had been asked was to spread a thin aura of respectability as chaperone for Ann, who was still married to Esmond Rothermere at this time. Ian and Ann used to leave in a small boat to fish or study the reef and not return until dusk, while I was left alone with no one to talk to and nowhere to go. I became drugged with boredom and lethargy and it was a happy day when Ivar Bryce turned up. He was a great friend of Ian's and in spite of Ian's cries of anguish and rage he insisted that we all dined out one night.

Some years later Ian asked a lady novelist out to stay but, knowing that Ann was very jealous, he did not pluck up the courage to tell her until it was too late to put the unfortunate lady off. After one day at Goldeneye it became clear that the situation was quite unbearable, so Ian took Noël Coward aside at lunch and begged him to take her to his house a few miles away. Noël agreed and then he said (in front of the unsuspecting lady), "Yes, I think I'll settle for the Polaroid camera."

Ian was very reluctant but saw that he had no choice. He grudgingly handed it over. Then there was a pause and Noël said, "And the tripod too." Again, poor Ian had to agree.

As the years went on the Flemings' life together deteriorated. Ann got cleverer and cleverer, while Ian, formerly the great star, did not advance. Ann's friends did not listen to him and he grew sulky. Finally he refused to go to her parties.

*C*yril Connolly in the garden at Send in 1943. A distinguished literary figure, and Editor of HORIZON, he became obsessed with the Happy Valley set in Kenya and the murder of Lord Erroll, since described in WHITE MISCHIEF, and could talk of nothing else.

*H*enry Weymouth (now Lord Bath) relaxing on the lawn. Longleat was the first stately home to open a safari park. People flock from miles around to see the lions there.

*W*raxhall Manor. From left to right: Me, Peter
Quennell, Clarissa Churchill, Ian Fleming, Middy
Gascoigne, Fionn O'Neill, Ann and Esmond
Rothermere.

*T*he library at Send Grove. Nicholas Lawford (the
former diplomat and painter who now lives in America)
standing by the books, myself, Sybil Colefax (the well
known – and often maligned hostess) and Peter
Quennell, the author.

The Salute at Venice in 1951. Myself, Grace Radziwill (now Dudley), Clarissa Churchill (who later married Anthony Eden), Stash Radziwill and Fred Warner (later Ambassador in Japan).

I was sent to Monte Carlo to cover Prince Rainier's wedding to Grace Kelly in April 1956 for a Sunday paper. It was the first time I saw the press behaving like savages. In the cathedral there were figures concealed behind every column and camera lenses emerging through the flowers. But the determination of the press was so intense that one cameraman literally stood on the altar and held on to the cross while he took aim. The service was ruined by endless flashlights. I had not been asked to the reception but Diana Cooper and Louise de Vilmorin saw no reason why I should be excluded. Thus firmly ensconced between them I sailed in passed the sentries. So to my great discomfort I became a gate-crasher for the first and only time in my life. The bride was very beautiful but I thought the bridesmaids' hats were hideous.

In Salzburg, I photographed Frau Wagner, with Chuck Turner. I did not know at the time she had been a close friend of Hitler and would have refused to shake her hand, had I done so.

On the same day, Fulco Verdura with the opera singer, Leontyne Price. Fulco was a Sicilian Duke, a painter and a jewellery designer who for several decades had an unrivalled influence on jewellery design. He had a shop in Fifth Avenue in New York and in Paris. I think of him as the Fabergé of his day.

*F*rom left to right: Hardy Amies, Victor Stiebel, Norman Hartnell, Yves St. Laurent, Madame Chauvel (wife of the French Ambassador), Lady Pamela Berry, Cecil Beaton. Standing at the back is Monsieur Jean Chauvel, the Ambassador, who was the host.

The occasion was a luncheon at the French Embassy to welcome the new young French dressmaker St. Laurent at the time of the Autumn Collections in about 1959 (Photo by William Lovelace).

*S*ir Michael Redgrave, the actor and director, with me at the opening of the Yvonne Arnaud Theatre in Guildford. I was a member of the theatre's board of directors for several years and was chairman of the Appeal executive.

*L*ord and Lady Rootes entertaining a shooting party at Ramsbury, the beautiful house sold to them by Lord Wilton. From left to right: Robert and Anne Rockley, Harold Macmillan (then Prime Minister), Anne and Billy Rootes, myself, John Wilton, Jackie Ward, and Geoffrey Rootes.

*M*y niece, Carolyn Ponsonby, then a model at Lanvin.

*D*ouglas Fairbanks Junior with his wife, Mary Lee, and daughters, Daphne, Melissa and Victoria. He is the son of Douglas Fairbanks (the swashbuckling hero of the silent films) and Mary Pickford. Douglas has been on screen since 1923, and is one of the great names of Hollywood.

*G*erald van der Kemp, curator of Versailles and the Trianons, whose many achievements in France have included the restoration of Monet's garden at Giverny, where he and his wife, Florence, live in the painter's flat and studio at weekends. Here he is in full evening dress.

A *Palm Beach group. From left to right: Me, Perla Mathieson, Kitty Miller (the hostess and wife of Gilbert Miller) and Alexis de Redé. Sybilla O'Donnell has her back to the camera.*

A *rare photograph indeed. The author Iris Murdoch prepares to try waterskiing in Corfu.*

I play cards with my previous publisher, George Weidenfeld.

Paul Reynaud, the brave Prime Minister of France, on a cruise arranged by Elsa Maxwell.

*O*livia de Havilland, the British-born actress and sister of Joan Fontaine and one of the stars of GONE WITH THE WIND, with "the Admiral" – Elsa Maxwell.

*C*ecil Beaton and I relaxing after dinner in Sam Wagstaff's apartment in New York in 1956.

Elsa Maxwell claimed she invented treasure hunts, which she did not, but she did invent scavenger hunts when you had to go in search of some weird object in the middle of the night, usually something awful like one of Mrs. Corrigan's wigs. She never had any money herself but she got money off rich people who wanted to get into society. Her great skill was that she could play any tune from any musical of the past fifty years on the piano. It was impossible to fault her. She would also be word perfect in the very latest Noël Coward or Cole Porter, and it was great fun listening to her. Once in New York she specified that tiaras should be worn at a huge party some millionaire was paying for. I am glad to say that none of the English wore them. Meanwhile Elsa borrowed the Empress Josephine's tiara from Van Cleef. It was about a foot high, made of magnificent diamonds, and I fear it was an incongruous sight to see her toad face underneath this glistening fender. She had enormous "joie de vivre" which sometimes spilt over to vulgarity.

*T*hree generations of Coopers – Diana, holding Jason, while John Julius (Norwich) looks on. The picture was taken at Chantilly.

A group in Nassau. From left to right: Anne Munroe, David Margesson, a pre-war Government Chief Whip, and Secretary of State for War from 1940 to 1942, with Sir Harold Christie, the man who found the body of Sir Harry Oakes in the famous murder case in the Bahamas in 1943. He developed the whole island which went from strength to strength as a tourist resort.

I was lucky enough to get a welcome lift home from St. Moritz with the Greek millionaire, Stavros Niarchos. We ate caviar and drank Dom Perignon for most of the flight back.

*J*udy Montagu (daughter of Asquith's confidante, Lady
Venetia Stanley, she later married Milton Gendel),
Lady Antonia Fraser (now Pinter), Daisy Fellowes (a
rich hostess), and John Galliher, a New Yorker.

*T*wo groups all dressed up for a ball at Wilton,
John Hope (now Lord Glendevon), Lady Essex, Cecil
Beaton, and Liza Hope (Lady Glendevon, and
daughter of Somerset Maugham).
At the table (clockwise) Cecil, Clementine Beit,
George Dix, Anne Norwich and Tony Pawson.

*S*ir John Betjeman, the Poet Laureate, taking a rest
from his labours in a summer garden.

Another group in Cecil Beaton's winter garden at Broadchalke, the day after the Wilton Ball.

Hardy Amies, dress designer to the Queen, and Fulco Verdura.

On a frightfully hot day in London in 1961, I was very late for lunch and just on the point of leaving my flat when the telephone rang. It was J. Walter Thompson with an astonishing query from Australia. They said they were looking for someone eminent in interior decoration to go on a lecture tour. I had never either lectured or decorated a house, though I had worked as a feature editor on HOUSE AND GARDEN *for some years. I protested it was impossible, but, gradually, I became interested and finally I succumbed. I prepared an erudite lecture for my six-week tour and delivered it with all its highbrow quotes to an audience who did not understand a word of it. I was staying with Sir Henry Abel Smith, Governor of Queensland, and his wife, Lady May, daughter of Princess Alice, Countess of Athlone, and I thought I must pull myself together. I had not come thousands of miles to be the worst-ever lecturer south of the Equator. So I threw away my notes and the painfully-learnt speech, and took heed of Diana Vreeland's advice never to talk down, but to be as one with your audience. I took the line that we were all at a jolly tea-party together and, from that moment on, things could not have gone better. I went to Darwin, Brisbane, Sydney, Melbourne, Adelaide and Perth, usually doing two lectures a day. I dreaded the appearances but loved the country. This photograph was taken in Brisbane. Perhaps the best part of all was spending my earnings on a glorious leisurely trip home, taking in rare sights such as Ankhor Wat and Pagan.*

I talk to Roderick More O'Ferrall, mounted for the hunt at Kildare, in Ireland.

*M*yself with my friends Jo and Ivar Bryce on board
the QUEEN ELIZABETH in 1956.

*S*etting off on one of my travels.

*V*anessa Redgrave before the opening of the Yvonne Arnaud Theatre. She borrowed a cap from a workman before accepting an invitation to plunge her foot into cement, leaving an imprint which theatre-goers can see to this day.

A portrait of me with one of my beloved schnauzers and a home-grown lily, in the library at Send Grove. I have had many generations of these little dogs.

*D*iana Cooper, Tom Parr (of Colefax and Fowler fame) and Fulco Verdura.

*M*e with Henry McIllhenny, that legendary host, who entertains not only in his magic castle, Glenveagh, in the wilds of Donegal, but also in Philadelphia and in Austria. As can be seen, we always have a good time.

My second husband, Sir Martin Lindsay of Dowhill, in the uniform of the Royal Company of Archers (The Queen's Bodyguard for Scotland).

*P*aul Getty with Martin at the Old Vicarage, Send.

*D*iana Mosley (one of the famous Mitford sisters) at
Cipriani's in Venice.

*A*n expedition from Schloss Prielau, the home of the
Hofmannsthals at Zell in Austria. Both Liz and
Raimund died far too young. From left to right: James
Lees-Milne (author and for many years adviser on
Historical Buildings for the National Trust), me,
Alvilde Lees-Milne, Liz, Diana Cooper, and
Raimund. Seated at the front is Alastair Forbes.

Princess Margaret arrived by helicopter on the lawn at Sutton Place and was greeted by Paul Getty and myself. She had come to a charity performance at the Yvonne Arnaud Theatre.

Cecil Beaton in informal mood on the lawn of the Old Vicarage at Send.

*T*he Queen Mother in my garden at Send in July
1971 with a group of friends. From left to right: Martin,
the Queen Mother, Pamela Lady Onslow, Lady Clare
Lindsay, Colonel Miles Reid, Oliver Lindsay,
Captain Alastair Aird, the Dowager Lady
Cholmondeley (formerly Sybil Sassoon), and Mrs.
Patrick Campbell-Preston (the Queen Mother's Lady
in Waiting).

*T*he Queen Mother at Send. She had attended a
grand lunch at Clandon and came over afterwards.

Aimée de Heeren, one of the most attractive women I ever knew.

Myself with Prince Tassilo Fürstenberg.

A recent photograph of me taken in March 1983. I am making friends with Peggy Willis's dog.

D iana Cooper in my garden at Send, then in her ninetieth year. Diana is now one of my oldest friends, but our friendship got off to a rather bad start. The Sitwells had made friends with her before the war and said she was just the sort of person I would love, so I looked forward to going to her cottage at Bognor to join a party for Goodwood. But, far from liking me, she practically snarled at me. Evidently she had been expecting Violet Westminster, who was a friend, and not unknown me. We soon overcame that poor start and became great friends. Among the many lessons I have learnt from her there was one unexpected one: she taught me how to make Pont l'Evêque cheese during the war. Later I often stayed at the Embassy in Paris.

PICTURE ACKNOWLEDGEMENTS

Photographs by Cecil Beaton on the bottom left of page 35, top of page 37, page 43, top left and bottom left of page 78, and the top of page 101 are by courtesy of Sotheby's Belgravia.
Grateful acknowledgement is made to the Condé Nast Publications Inc. for permission to reproduce drawings from Vogue *(1927) on page 36; and to Louise Dahl-Wolfe for permission to reproduce her photograph of Loelia, Duchess of Westminster on the bottom right of page 94.*

INDEX

OF PEOPLE